BETRAYAL AND INTRIGUE WEAVE A SHOCKING WEB OF DECEIT

MURDER IN MINNESOTA

CITY OF MINNETONKA

JOHN FILCHER

ISBN: 978-1-962402-14-9

Published by

Fideli Publishing, Inc.
119 W. Morgan St.
Martinsville, IN 46151
www.FideliPublishing.com

ACKNOWLEDGMENTS

For my family, this book series (and hopefully more to come) was only possible because my eldest daughter wanted to be represented in a fictional book. Preferably as a villainess. Request granted, but, like all my children, the character is much more complex than that. Special thanks to Frances, my editor, without whom this work would have given a whole new meaning to the term "rough draft."

MURDER IN MINNESOTA

CITY OF MINNETONKA

CHAPTER 1

The man's cold, gray eyes were set in a chiseled face framed by salt-and-pepper hair visible under his dark brown fedora. Those cold eyes scrutinized my face from across the small table in a local brewpub named after an 1800s era Supreme Court case, *United States v. Forty-Three Gallons of Whiskey*.

Maintaining a disciplined radio silence, I kept my Game Face in place and stared right back at Jacob Archer. Knowing from prior experience that he disliked mixed messages, this was the blankest look I could muster while still conveying my displeasure. A bead of sweat born from the effort of carefully controlling my expression traced a path down my face, causing my left eye to twitch as the salty droplet rolled past.

"Make your move," said Archer gruffly, his steely eyes attempting to bore holes into my soul as he looked for a sign of weakness. A crusty, retired detective from the Prior Lake Police Department, Archer's brand new, gray mustache twitched as he concentrated.

Obliging Archer, I moved. A quick double jump, and my red checker landed at his end of the board. "King that," I said with a humorless half-smile that was mostly hidden by my new salt-and-pepper beard.

"Bastard," Archer grunted as he crowned the offending game piece with a second layer before taking his own turn and jumping another red checker in the middle of the board. He was trying to draw my defense out into the open.

Movement caught Archer's attention, drawing his gaze to someone passing behind me before his focus returned to the game board. Intertwining his fingers, Archer leaned closer to the board as though he were closely studying the unfolding strategy being played out on it.

"On your six, Dante," Archer noted so quietly his voice would have been drowned out had I not been locked in and listening intently. Intertwining his fingers and leaning slightly over the game board was our prearranged signal to indicate he was going to say something for my ears only. As it was, the noise level of the busy brew pub this evening ensured no one could overhear us.

Casually leaning back, I surveyed the crowd in Forty-Three Gallons of Whiskey Brewing Company while taking a sip of an amber lager called Trial by Fire. Raising my eyebrows in appreciation of its rich taste and smooth finish, I grunted in approval while indirectly observing Ryan Anderson as he sat down at a reserved table directly in my line of sight. At the adjoining table sat my daughter Riley and my son-in-law Jeffrey.

Archer and I continued our battle for checkers supremacy in silence while we waited to see what transpired next. Sighing, Archer sat more upright and cracked his neck before taking a sip of his own brew. He was drinking a thick, dark beer and he glanced with a questioning look.

"Why is this beer called Pro Foama? What does that even mean?" Archer asked.

Shrugging slightly, I responded, "It's a play on the legal phrase *pro forma*, which means "as a matter of form." But since its beer, they went with foama to be cutesy."

Snorting softly in disgust, Archer just shook his head and frowned. "Lawyers just have to ruin everything, don't they? Even beer."

Stifling a laugh at Archer's expense, I glanced at the game board again. "If only you knew," I said before abruptly changing subjects. "She's here," I whispered as I reached for another red checker.

"With the subject?" Archer asked, raising his eyebrows slightly as he pretended to study our game.

"Oh yes. Sitting across from him now. Crocodile tears in her eyes."

Our quarry was Samantha Triton, the socialite wife of the billionaire industrialist Martin Triton. Not long ago, Mr. Triton had been imprisoned for murdering his rival, Bill Harrison. Now, Mrs. Triton was seated with the longtime security chief of Triton Industries, Ryan Anderson. They were arguing and she appeared to be pleading with Ryan.

Without looking up from the game board, Archer cocked an eyebrow and said, "Lovers' quarrel?"

Following Archer's lead, I rubbed my chin while staring at the board and nodded slightly. "Yep. No doubt he just told her about his Dead Man's Switch to protect himself from her murderous ways."

"If she finds a way around that," Archer calmly noted, "Anderson will become a corpse."

Anderson's melodramatically named Dead Man Switch would, in the event of his untimely demise, result in disclosing information substantiating Samantha Triton's crimes to the media. The meeting we were now witnessing was Anderson's way of proving the truth of information he had secretly accumulated about Samantha Triton's crimes while posing as her lover.

Unbeknownst to Mrs. Triton, the media *already* possessed that information. Anderson had delivered it to my daughter Annabelle earlier in the day, and she was already prepping the corresponding episode of Murder in Minnesota to air all of Samantha's dirty laundry.

"Riley and Jeffrey still in position?" Archer asked.

My eyes flicked past our quarry to the table next to Triton and Anderson. "Yep. They're pretending to play cards. Riley just rubbed her finger along the top of her nose to indicate they're listening in on the conversation."

"I can't believe these stupid disguises actually worked," Archer grumbled. "I hate false mustaches."

I sighed softly. "At least *you* didn't have to go with a full beard like me. Makes me want to scratch my face off." My eyes glanced past Triton and Anderson instead of focusing directly on them. They were still in a heated discussion. "The rich and powerful never seem to notice us senior citizen types," I added.

"Unless you're a rich and powerful senior citizen," Archer added as he moved a checker.

Archer and I knew we both had a lot of work to do.

CHAPTER 2

"Jerry, I dunno. Taking on billionaires is a whole different animal than the government," noted Annabelle between sips of the dark red wine she was enjoying.

My 31-year-old daughter, Annabelle Masterson, was sitting on the couch as our team ate dinner in her living room. Annabelle took a bite of steak burrito, which I had brought from my friend, Paul, who owns the El Burro Azul food truck that ranges throughout the south metro. Her flaming red hair and blue eyes reflected the dying light of the setting sun coming through the kitchen window at the far end of the great room, which included both the kitchen and living room.

After corrupt government officials derailed the investigation of the murder of Zoe Finch, Annabelle was understandably skittish at the prospect of making powerful new enemies. Thankfully the sleazy civil servants who absolutely bungled their prosecution of Annabelle had been exposed when Annabelle's case went to the jury. The trumped-up show trial over Zoe Finch's murder and mutilated body parts scattered around Prior Lake in a deranged scavenger hunt that widely became known as Bimbo Bits, resulting in a scandal and media firestorm that propelled

Annabelle's investigative "Murder in Minnesota" podcast into national prominence. Ending the tyrannical careers of meddling kleptocrats was seen by the public as a bonus when Annabelle's freedom was restored by way of her victory in trial.

"Murder in Minnesota" had earned a reputation for uncovering all sorts of interesting facts about murders around the state. The podcast not only revealed those undisclosed investigative facts to the public — it exposed bureaucratic malfeasance and prompted the reversal of murder convictions on appeal when its revelations established a defendant's innocence.

The program's growing prominence required more resources to continue its good work and expanded operations. That expansion included Jacob Archer. He is a man with the natural instinct to do what is right as best he can, yet underneath that armored exterior beats the heart of an experienced cynic who knows life is messy and usually involves shortcuts somewhere. Archer was the detective who had investigated the Zoe Finch murder. The expansion also included me, a retired corporate attorney in addition to being Annabelle's dad. While Archer and I shared a complicated history from his prior investigation of Annabelle, we worked unexpectedly well together and were now close friends. It was unclear which of us was more surprised by that. Trial attorney Jerry Tavington, who handles the legal matters involving "Murder in Minnesota," was the final member of the primary team. My son and other daughter, and their respective spouses, are often called in to provide support as needed.

"It's not so much we're taking on billionaires. One of them is asking for our help," replied Tavington, speaking through a mouthful of fish taco.

Snorting, Archer said, "Yeah, a *convicted* billionaire. To investigate his murder conviction for ending a rival billionaire." He was lounging in the brown leather chair next to the fireplace and washed down a bite of steak nachos with a drink of nut-brown ale.

I put down my chicken fajita burrito and looked at Archer. "Just because he's rich doesn't mean he didn't get screwed by the system. Maybe the worst we can do is look into a high-profile trial, shine some light into the dark places, and ask some awkward questions? Even if nothing changes, it's got some interesting components to talk about on the show."

"Components like the billionaire's gorgeous wife?" Annabelle asked with a sly smile creeping across her face. She loved salacious gossip.

Archer barked a short laugh. "Samantha Triton seems pretty dreamy on the surface. Drop-dead gorgeous former model. Children's book author. Philanthropist. And she's even a world-renowned gardener."

I arched my right eyebrow while half-smiling. "And you're, uh, looking to prune her roses or something?"

"Dad!" exclaimed Annabelle with an annoyed look on her face. Tavington spit out a chunk of half-chewed fish taco while trying to stifle a roar of laughter.

Archer smirked. "All I'm saying is she is the kind of intriguing character people want to learn more about. Not too many rich, glamorous gals in their early 40s out there with billionaire husbands serving a life sentence for murdering their rival."

Nodding, I said, "Hard to argue with that, especially when that rich hubby wants us to look into his situation. Plenty of rumors floating around out there about Samantha catting around on Martin before the trial."

"And he pays well! Kind of a bonus for once," Annabelle noted wryly. Normally "Murder in Minnesota" relied on advertising revenues, which had been plentiful since Annabelle beat the rap in the Zoe Finch murder trial. Getting paid specifically to dig up dirt was something new for us.

"Sounds like it's time to vote. Who wants to look into Martin of Minnetonka's circumstances?" I asked. With four drinks raised high, there was no need to ask for votes against taking on the job.

CHAPTER 3

"**M**r. Finch, Mr. Archer, thank you for coming, gentlemen. Please follow me to Mr. Triton's office," said the receptionist as she motioned towards our destination with a sweeping arm gesture. Correctly assuming we would follow, she started walking down the hall to the executive suite of Triton Industries.

Trailing behind her, Archer looked skeptically at me and silently mouthed, "Gentleman? You?"

Arching an eyebrow, I glanced imperiously at Archer's choice of clothing before meeting his eyes. Too softly for the receptionist to hear, I muttered, "You look like a fed posing as a mad professor in a cheap B movie."

Pretending to brush specks of dust from the arm of his tweed sport coat, Archer snorted softly at my critical opinion of his fashion sense. We trailed behind the receptionist to a door she held open for us.

Waiting in the large office was Terry Triton, who immediately rose and walked around his empty desk to shake hands with us. "Thank you for coming to see me. Shall we?" he said, motioning with his arm towards an equally empty conference table.

In his early 30s, Triton was a man of average height and build with black hair and piercing blue eyes. A decade earlier he graduated from the University of Minnesota with degrees in mathematics and business, and now was the heir apparent to Triton Industries.

After coffees were poured and we were alone, Terry spoke. "What do you two know about my father's murder conviction?"

Trading quick glances with me, Archer responded first. "Martin was the head of Triton Industries here in Minnetonka when he was convicted of poisoning his rival Bill Harrison in a highly publicized trial. Subsequent to that, your stepmother Samantha Triton took control of the day-to-day operations of the company. Your father's legal appeals were unsuccessful. He is serving a life sentence with no possibility of parole."

Nodding, Triton said, "All true. Would you believe me if I say there's more to it than that?"

"There's been all sorts of rumors swirling around the trial since day one. Can you walk us through which ones you are getting at?" I asked. I didn't want to blindly go chasing rumors. That sort of thing just wasn't a productive use of our time.

"I think if you look into her, Sam isn't what she seems to be," Triton said enigmatically.

Trading glances with me again, Archer asked, "In what way? Can you clarify?"

Shrugging, Triton glanced above and away from us as he composed his thoughts for a moment. Returning his eyes to Archer, Triton responded, "My working theory is that she engineered my father's incarceration to take control of the company. I don't know how. She is very manipulative and always seems to get what she wants."

Startled, I asked, "Wait, you aren't in control of the company yet?"

Shaking his head, Triton said, "No. I'm just a board member. Someday I'll inherit my father's shares and control of the company but for now, Sam is in control of his shares." Triton went on to state a few more things that didn't make sense to him.

Soon, Archer and I returned to our vehicle in the company parking lot and departed. A mile or two passed while we collected our thoughts in silence. Archer, in the passenger seat, spoke first. "Something about this situation seems more 'off' than you expected?"

Nodding, I glanced at him with my right eyebrow raised quizzically. "Yeah. More than just a simple dynamic of a corporate power struggle going on here." I then looked directly at him, "We're going to need to get together with Samantha Triton and take her temperature about us looking into Martin's conviction."

Archer pursed his lips slightly and nodded in agreement. "It'll be informative to see how that plays out."

* * *

"I'm so glad you made the time to see me. I have some tea and snacks waiting in the sunroom," Samantha Triton said after introductions. Archer, Annabelle and I followed her through the opulent Triton mansion, which occupied several lakefront lots on Lake Minnetonka that had previously been the sites of several modest homes. Not that Archer or I could have afforded even the "modest" predecessors, much less the current stately abode that Mrs. Triton reportedly had designed herself. It was a sprawling structure that provided lake views from multiple rooms. The price of the combined 3-acre lakefront lot was $15 million, which didn't even factor in the cost of the 12,000-square-foot residence which had been designed to look a century older than it actually was.

Arm in arm with Annabelle, Mrs. Triton led the conversation while guiding us through the large home. Besides being beautiful, she was charming in a way that mostly seemed natural. "I have been following your show, "Murder in Minnesota," ever since you were arrested for the murder of your distant relative. It's a fantastic production. So juicy! Your exposure of those awful, corrupt prosecutors was the greatest tell-all I've ever heard," she said.

While Annabelle and Mrs. Triton engaged in light conversation, Archer and I tried our best to look at everything without seeming to look at anything as we trailed behind. Extravagance was everywhere. The light fixtures alone undoubtedly cost more than both my vehicles, combined.

We soon found ourselves seated in what Mrs. Triton airily called the sunroom. It was a large indoor garden surrounding an elevated, glass-walled sitting room positioned atop the outer wall of the garden structure. Bathed in direct sunshine, the room commanded dramatic views of both the indoor and exterior garden, and of Lake Minnetonka just beyond the outdoor grounds. Filled with comfortable furniture, the sunroom was a bright place of climate-controlled comfort and relaxation that complimented Mrs. Triton's effervescent and vivacious personality. The lengthy runs of glass wall facing the lake that also provided sound-proofed privacy from being overheard in the indoor garden, had to cost a $1 million or more.

"How can I help your investigation?" Mrs. Triton suddenly asked after tea had been served and the pleasantries dispensed with. "Are you trying to find some way to get Martin out of jail?" Her eyes briefly blazed with a direct intensity as she seemingly tried to stare into Annabelle's soul. As quickly as that intensity appeared, it vanished again behind the pleasant facade we had originally encountered.

The abrupt change in Mrs. Triton's demeanor was jarring and caused me to wonder whether she was concealing a more calculated intention behind her seemingly innocent question. Trading glances with Archer, I could see his internal alarm had also triggered. His left eyebrow twitched slightly, which I had learned was an unconscious tell that something was off but he wasn't sure what it was yet.

Using an old conversation technique, Annabelle had already decided to mirror Mrs. Triton's animated warmth, not letting on that she had similarly observed Mrs. Triton's subtle change in tone. "Oh, it's been a *very* interesting story for us! And we simply couldn't turn down an invitation to look inside and find an angle to tell that hasn't already been told ..."

"Oh, honey!" Mrs. Triton sweetly interrupted. "It's been just hideous to live through! But I was wondering, who asked for more news coverage at this late date?"

To my ears, Mrs. Triton spoke of her husband's conviction too super-ficially, almost as though it had been a mere inconvenience—like retelling a story about a treacherous drive down one of Minnesota's snow-covered roads that her personal driver had navigated—rather than a life-altering event that touched her personally.

Annabelle was the picture of warmth and concern for Mrs. Triton as she replied, "Your stepson, Terry, invited our team in to see if we could run a series on the murder and conviction. While he is giving us total access to anyone or anything, he also suggested we obtain your blessing first."

Mrs. Triton hesitated slightly before responding. It wasn't much and was unlikely to be noticed by someone not watching for it. "Well, I for one am glad Terry wants you to get to the bottom of this. This has been such a trying time for all of us. Please let me know if there is anything at all that I can do to help."

Soon, our meeting with Mrs. Triton concluded and we piled into my pickup for the ride back to Prior Lake. Annabelle broke the silence first.

"Oh my God! What WAS that?" she exclaimed. Archer and I traded sly glances and half-smiles that lacked any humor.

"The creepy part, or the other creepy part?" Archer asked. Despite the vagueness of his witty question, Annabelle knew exactly what Archer meant.

"The whole, creepy, charm offensive part!" Annabelle said, with an exaggerated shudder. "THEN the creepy, 'boo-hoo, my poor husband,' part. What the hell *was* that? She must get tired, putting makeup on her two faces every morning," Annabelle groused.

Nodding, Archer snorted a laugh. "At least you took the brunt of all that. Me and Dante were just the hired help to her." Archer and I often threw Annabelle under the figurative bus to absorb someone's attention and free us up to do our thing. By now, she was both used to it and it had become an old joke among us.

Now it was my turn to laugh as I wove through the light traffic on Highway 169. Thankfully, rush hour hadn't started yet. "Typical social climber type. Only acknowledge your existence when they think they'll need something from you, then ghost you until the next time. Had a VP like that once back in the day. Total clown, everybody else saw right through her phony act."

My eyes flicked to check the rear-view mirror again. "We have a tail," I noted. "Black SUV."

Nobody turned around to look because Archer had the foresight to train us in advance, ensuring we were too savvy to make rookie mistakes like that.

Archer didn't question my accuracy in spotting a tail. He started the video recording function on his cellphone and carefully slid it behind the rear seat headrest in my truck. "Your windows are tinted dark enough that I don't think they could see me sliding the phone into place," he said.

We drove in silence for several minutes as I casually changed lanes a few times to give us the best chance of capturing the SUV on the video, making it seem as if I were merely passing slow drivers. At last Archer pulled the phone back and watched the video for a few moments. "We got it," he said. "Take the next exit and drive to the Edina police station."

Our tail tried to inconspicuously follow us through the suburban traffic, trying to keep several vehicles behind my truck. The driver hesitated briefly when he or she saw us pulling into a police station and then they continued on. Once our tail was out of sight, I quickly exited the parking lot and headed in a different direction before the tail could return and resume following us.

"Car's registered to Erik Johnson of Maple Grove," Archer said, reading the message on his phone.

"You found out who it is already?" Annabelle asked in disbelief.

Archer shook his head. "No, just who owns the vehicle. They never got close enough for us to ID a driver."

"Clearly that direct access to DMV for vehicle registration information was a good investment," I quipped. "Shall we visit the good Mr. Johnson?"

"Tomorrow?" Archer asked.

Nodding, I said, "Yeah, unless something else comes up. I want to see if we can dig up anything on him first."

An hour later, after dropping Archer and Annabelle off at their places, I pulled into my garage. I abruptly stopped my truck halfway in when I noticed an envelope on the garage floor. I was certain it hadn't been there before.

"Shit," I muttered as I put the truck in park, retrieved the envelope and then pulled all the way into the garage. I knew what an envelope on my garage floor meant. It was the preferred method my mysterious "friend" used to let me know I should call the number on a slip of paper in the envelope. The number was different each time I received a note, and I already knew my home security cameras would only show a hooded person walking up to my garage to slip the envelope under the door.

I had given that hooded person the name "Word Man." I don't know his real name, and he doesn't know I had dubbed him Word Man. I'm pretty sure Word Man's employer is a drug kingpin or cartel boss of some sort. Last year, Mysterious Friend dispatched Word Man and another henchman, whom I call Scar Man, to deliver a message to me. As I was making my way home during a heavy snowstorm after visiting an old friend who was serving time at the federal prison camp near Duluth, Word Man and Scar Man trapped my car between theirs. Their "request" was that I inform my incarcerated friend, who happened to be a former bookkeeper of said kingpin's organization, that speaking about his work would put his sister's family in danger.

Even though I met him just that once, I remember Word Man well. He had swarthy skin and black hair that was turning gray. His black eyes, which were framed by crow's-feet, looked emotionless and dead. They did not seem to be eyes that reflected any humor from within whatsoever. The way Word Man speaks, I have zero difficulty believing he is the kind of man who was experienced in making sure people follow through with promises.

I had made a hollow promise to pass their message along to my friend in prison in exchange for future favors, but initially I wasn't bright enough to follow through. Now I harbor a strong suspicion that the gruesome murder of Zoe Finch, my mooching distant relative, was their way of making sure I understood I should do what I was told.

One thing I now know for sure, my Mysterious Friend is quite serious about following through with promises in both directions. When I later had to call in a favor from Mysterious Friend, his interventions quickly resulted in aborting the prosecution of Annabelle.

I was both stunned and impressed by my Mysterious Friend's actions, yet, like the old saying goes, "With friends like these, who needs enemies." I had no idea how to be rid of this friend, and I was always afraid of what I would be asked to do. So far, the "ask" has been less scary than the consequences of failing to perform what he asked of me.

CHAPTER 4

"Erik Johnson worked at Triton Industries," Archer said. "Makes me wonder who had him tail us."

"Seriously?" I said in surprise. I hadn't known where Johnson had worked. "Not often we get tailed by a corpse." I took a sip of my coffee to give Archer a moment to process the bombshell I just dropped.

Now it was Archer's turn to be surprised. "Corpse?" he said with a confused look. "What are you talking about?"

"Erik Johnson's corpse was found floating in Lake Minnetonka a couple months ago. Somebody ended him and robbed his place. I found the probate paperwork filed online with the court." I didn't need to explain to Archer that the civil judiciary's tech system often didn't mesh well with law enforcement's, so information and data needed to be searched independently. Which is why we hadn't found the same data.

Archer leaned back in his chair as sunlight filtered through my kitchen window spilled across the table. We'd decided to meet at my place to start our day of sleuthing by hatching out a few schemes, which is a more interesting way of saying we were having coffee and trying to figure out what is going on.

A small, red-headed girl dressed in jammies with little baseballs and bats printed on them came bounding down the hall from the front stairs and immediately commanded our attention. She ran with that cute, side-to-side gait that toddlers everywhere have and squealed in excitement at being chased by my daughter, Riley.

"I'm gonna get youuuu!" Riley said in a singsong as she threatened to catch my granddaughter, Mary, who careened full speed into my outstretched arms.

"Papa! Hide me!" Mary squealed between giggles. She squirmed in closer, as if she could suddenly disappear from Riley's view by burying herself in my arms. It didn't work.

"Got you!" Riley exclaimed, lifting her squirming little prey into her arms like a victorious hunter. Mary exploded with laughter when Riley blew a raspberry on Mary's tummy, which stuck out of her jammies.

Archer and I chuckled as Riley chased Mary back upstairs to get her dressed.

"Never a dull moment here. They have any luck finding a house yet?" Archer asked, tilting his head down the hall that Riley and Mary had disappeared into.

Taking another sip of my steaming coffee, I nodded. "Yep. Their offer on a new place over by the west side of Spring Lake was accepted by the builder last night. They'll be moved in by fall," I explained. Archer already knew Riley and Jeffrey had decided to relocate from Charleston to this area, but he hadn't yet heard if they had found a house. It wasn't easy to find a house in Prior Lake because it is a desirable suburb in the Twin Cities metro, and Spring Lake was the largest lake in the suburb.

My wife, Heidi, and I were very pleased to have our middle child and her family move closer to the rest of us. Even though Riley hated cold weather, it turns out she hates hurricanes even more. The last flooding event from a hurricane had proven to be the straw that broke the camel's back, so they were moving to Minnesota. My other two kids, Annabelle and Joel, were always excited for their sibling to come home and now my house was pretty busy with all the kids, their spouses, and my grandchildren trooping through it.

Turning serious, Archer looked at me and asked, "So, the question is, who was following us and why?"

Looking away at nothing in particular, I thought about it for a moment. "Because the ownership of the vehicle is someone we can already loosely connect to Martin Triton by virtue of where he was employed, at a minimum I'm thinking that probably eliminates any players from other investigations. So, we start with the obvious …"

Nodding, Archer completed the thought. "We look for connections between Johnson and Triton. My thoughts exactly. Do some in-depth homework on Johnson first and regroup tomorrow?"

"Yeah. I have an errand to run in the morning, so maybe late afternoon?"

"Perfect," said Archer.

* * *

"Solid Waste, Inc." were the only words visible on the aging, rusty sign on the outside of a ratty old brick building in the gritty warehouse district of the downtown metro. My errand now had me standing in front of the decrepit entrance and from what I could see no one else was around. Above the door was a battered, ancient light sconce that probably would do little more than cast weak light over the entry. It felt somewhat fortunate to visit during the daylight hours as I had little doubt this was no place to be at night. The hardscrabble old industrial vibe of the district did not provide any clarity on whether it was more, or less, safe to be here alone.

I fished my burner phone from the pocket of my pants and opened the app that was now on this phone. Normally I keep the apps on a phone, burner or personal, to a bare minimum for security purposes but this particular application had possibilities that were intriguing. It was an unnamed app that could track cell phone signals and filter them based on characteristics like distance, speed and altitude. Installing it required jail breaking the phone's operating system and downloading the software directly from a server somewhere out on the dark web. Applying the filter, I looked at the results on the screen. *Still there*, I thought.

I decided to open the door and enter anyway. It led to a small, poorly lit, filthy waiting room that had seen better days several decades ago. Next to a security door on the wall opposite the main entrance was a window that appeared to be a former ticket booth. It was one of those windows with a round speaking hole at face height, and a gap at the bottom for sliding money or keys underneath. Staring back at me through that window was a decidedly unfriendly looking face.

The face belonged to a heavyset, unshaven guy in his mid-40s who was wearing a white, stained, wife beater t-shirt, the kind you tend to see on "reality" TV when cameras follow police officers into a trailer park. He was the kind of man who had a 5 o'clock shadow by lunchtime and, from the look of his hairy arms and shoulders, bench pressed truck engines for fun. Saying nothing, he slowly chewed the remains of an unlit cigar. His face betrayed little besides being decidedly unimpressed by a visitor to Solid Waste, Inc.

Must've gotten Bruno here from the leftover dregs in Central Casting, I thought. *He fits every stereotype in the book for shady places of business.*

Without smiling, I stepped up to the window and said, "Good morning. I'm here to see Mr. Sorvino." I didn't mention to this guy that I had just dubbed him "Bruno" in my head.

The cigar slowly rolled from the left to the right side of his mouth while Bruno quietly considered what I just said before removing the cigar. "And who might you be, boy?" he asked, pointing with the stub of the cigar that was now lodged between his fingers. His raspy, guttural voice probably sounded threatening even when he was in a good mood. Bruno clearly wasn't in a good mood.

"A friend."

"Sorvino ain't got no friends like you, Mr. Fancypants. Get the fuck outta here," Bruno snarled.

Annoyed, I decided it was time to take control of the situation and start speaking Bruno's language. "Maybe he's got friends that he didn't know he has. Fuck with me again and you'll be pushing up daisies out in the woods somewhere." Naturally gravelly, my deep bass voice began sounding like a cross between a hate crime and rock crusher when I got annoyed.

Before Bruno could return fire, the security door was opened by Mr. Sorvino. He was every bit as pleasant as Bruno.

"Who da fuck are you?" Sorvino asked brusquely.

My silent response surprised both Sorvino and Bruno. With my index finger, I pointed towards the ceiling, then tapped my ear with it before motioning for everyone to remain silent. Both men unexpectedly got the message, and said nothing. I silently mimed writing a note in my hand then pointed towards the pen and notepad inside the window by Bruno. He handed both to me.

I scribbled a message to Sorvino. "Drone surveillance outside now. Remain silent." Both men read it then handed it back to me.

Writing quickly, I penned out the message. *Our mutual friend in the trade says to tell you the feds are watching and you need to be like a fox instead of a lion.* I showed it to Sorvino, who nodded. His demeanor had changed entirely and he was now paying very close attention to what I was writing. Sorvino motioned for me to hand him the notepad and pen.

"How do I know I can trust you?" Sorvino wrote.

I slowly brought the burner phone from my pocket and unlocked the screen. The unnamed app was active, so I handed it to Sorvino. I motioned to return the pad and pen. *Cell phone tracking shows a drone with a cell phone is outside. The control signals are coming from two blocks over,* I wrote.

Alarmed, I saw Bruno suddenly duck inside the backdoor leading from the ticket booth into the space beyond. Within seconds, he burst through the thick metal security door carrying a semi-auto shotgun and quickly stormed through the front door to the outside of the building. Sorvino and I exchanged a silent glance when we heard three blasts in rapid succession.

Within a minute, Bruno reappeared through the front door. He was carrying the remains of a small surveillance drone in his left hand, while the right held the shotgun pointed towards the ceiling. Bruno handed the junked drone to Sorvino and turned to lock the front entrance.

Without a word, Sorvino looked at me and pointed towards the security door next to the booth with a nod of his head. I followed him into the space beyond. As we passed into the dimly lit hallway, it became apparent that the metal security door was solid steel and about 2 inches thick. It looked like it could stop a battering ram. The hallway beyond revealed a closed door leading to the ticket booth and more doorways further down that were barely visible in the dim, yellowed lighting.

Bruno slammed the metal security door behind us and locked it. He ran to catch up with Sorvino and me.

"We got about 15 minutes before the feds bust through that door, Boss. I'll get everyone moving," Bruno said.

Wordlessly, the three of us entered the last room on the left and Bruno shut the door behind us. It appeared to be a little used supply room that was dimly lit by a single bulb hanging down on a frayed cord from the ceiling. The dirty brick walls of the room were lined by shelves filled with old machinery parts and strongly smelled of old oil and grease. I was growing nervous about what was going to happen to me in this room, but was soon surprised when Sorvino grabbed the far shelf with both hands and pulled. Despite its outward appearance, the heavy shelf quietly swung inwards on a hidden bracket to reveal a trapdoor in the floor.

Opening the trapdoor, Bruno led the way down followed by Sorvino. When I didn't immediately follow, Sorvino popped his head back up through the opening and said, "You wanna be a guest of the feds, or make like a shadow? Pull the door closed behind you and the shelf will swing back over the hole and the lock will engage." Then he disappeared back down.

Sorvino was right. To say the least, it would be awkward to try to explain away my presence here to the feds, especially after Bruno blew their drone out of the sky. I quickly secured the trapdoor back into place behind me and heard a lock click shut. The steep, narrow steps lacked a handrail, and the three of us put our hands on the dark brick walls for balance as we clambered down at least three stories underground. These hidden stairs were probably built over a century ago, and whoever made them certainly had been less concerned with safety than secrecy.

Whatever I expected to find at the bottom wasn't what was there after Sorvino opened a door on the final landing and walked through. Instead of a dank, musty old underground secret entrance there was a speakeasy, a richly decorated entertaining suite complete with a well-stocked bar and a series of rooms adjoining a long hallway. I continued to follow Sorvino and Bruno through the speakeasy into a long, dimly lit hall that disappeared into the darkness ahead. They opened at least a dozen doors along the way to tell the occupants it was time to skedaddle.

As the hall quickly filled with people headed out, we then walked into the last room. By now, I thought nothing else was going to surprise me too much today. Wrong again.

Inside was a threesome, with an attractive, middle-aged blonde mounted atop some guy with an armful of tattoos while another tattooed guy made a meat sandwich with her as the middle. They were less than half her age. While they kept grinding, Sorvino turned to me with a serious look on his face. "Do me a favor?"

Eyes meeting Sorvino's, I simply replied, "Anywhere but here."

Finding that answer satisfactory, Sorvino nodded and a half-smile briefly ghosted across his face while the threesome arrived at the conclusion of their festivities. "Mrs. Kettle over there needs a ride home. Can you do that?"

"Will do." My answer was short and to the point. Glancing at who I surmised was Mrs. Kettle, I watched her dismount and the threesome began to dress quickly.

"Thanks. Follow the herd the rest of the way to the end of the hall, then take the steps up to street level. It's a hike, but you'll be several blocks away by then." Sorvino turned to the two men who had been entertaining Mrs. Kettle and motioned for them to precede us out of the room.

Mrs. Kettle sidled up to me as she shrugged up her skirt, turning her back to me. "Zip me up, honey?"

Ever the gentleman, I naturally obliged. Kettle appeared to be in her late 50s, with blonde hair that I figured was an excellent dye job to hide any gray. She turned to face me after her skirt was zipped up, and she suddenly pulled me closer and planted a seductive kiss on my lips. Her sudden kiss completely startled me.

Pulling away, Kettle said in a hungry voice, "Oh, I love shy men." It was unclear what drugs she had taken to cause the red rimming of her eyes, but it now accentuated their bright blue color.

Motioning toward the exit with a small wave of my arm, I simply looked at Kettle and said, "Time to go."

By now, the long, dimly lit brick hallway leading from the speakeasy was empty. We hurried towards the end, which was shrouded by darkness. We found ourselves reemerging topside through a nondescript exit with a heavy, rusted door into bright daylight bathing a little used side street. As described by Sorvino, we had traveled several blocks underground, undetected by the feds who had been watching the speakeasy underneath the grimy facade of Solid Waste, Inc.

Soon I was again behind the wheel of my black pickup truck, headed west on I-394. In the front passenger seat was Mrs. Kettle, blinking her red-rimmed eyes to try to adjust to the bright sunshine.

"Tammy," she said quietly by way of introducing herself a bit more.

Glancing at her, I said, "Pleasure to meet you, Tammy." I pointedly did not give her a name, real or otherwise. I also hadn't provided a name to Sorvino or Bruno.

Despite being high as a kite, Tammy figured out the message that it is better not to know anything about me and simply provided an address in Minnetonka where I should deliver her. About a half-hour later, we entered an exclusive neighborhood around Lake Minnetonka that I recognized. As we passed by the entrance to a familiar mansion, Tammy broke our silence by pointing towards it and saying, "There's Samantha's house. She's very good between the sheets."

Obviously, Tammy was still stoned, but now my curiosity was getting the better of me. "Mrs. Triton and you?"

Looking at me with an awkwardly intoxicated tilt of her head, Tammy said, "Oh yeah. Sam is talented with both women AND men. Since she got Martin out of the house, she's doing anybody she wants. Sam and I have been humping Mr. Ryan since before then."

I turned into a driveway several homes away from Samantha Triton's and put the truck's transmission into park. Even though I was sure I would regret it, I had to ask. "Who's Mr. Ryan?"

Tammy leaned over to me and wrapped an arm behind my neck. Whispering into my right ear, she quietly said, "Ryan Anderson." Then her tongue snaked out to my ear and she got my ear lobe between her lips before I could react.

Lustily whispering now, Tammy said, "Come inside. I got more sugar for you, baby. My husband is out of town again."

It was instantly apparent that this was the best opportunity I'd have all day, so I took it. Shaking my head, I said, "Can't, ma'am. I'm taken, and I got places to be." It was time to get the hell out of this situation and be anywhere else but here, and this was the perfect moment to make a break for it.

"I'll be waiting," Tammy said, blowing a kiss my way and sliding out the door of the truck. She unsteadily sauntered up the rest of the driveway to her own mansion as I watched and sighed in relief.

I drove to a nearby park and backed the truck under a tree at the far edge of the parking lot with a line of overgrown shrubs and hedges that obscured what I was about to do. Opening the trunk hidden under the bed of the truck, I removed a power screwdriver and second set of license plates I stashed inside before today's field trip to the realm of the underworld. Within minutes, my black truck again bore its real license plates while the fake plates and screwdriver were put away out of sight in the trunk.

By the time I got on Highway 169 to drive south back to Prior Lake, my mind was replaying the crazy events of the past 90 minutes. I hadn't expected today's errand would lead to Sorvino's underground speakeasy, drug den and cheap sex emporium. Nor had I expected the highly unattractive offer of thirsty thirds with a heavily stoned, drop-dead gorgeous blonde woman in her late 50s right after I had witnessed the completion of her lurid threesome with a couple of tattooed guys in their 20s.

All of that was surprising, but none of it compared to the revelation that Mrs. Kettle and Mrs. Triton were well acquainted with each other and someone named Ryan Anderson. It was impossible to ignore that my errand for the Mysterious Friend and our investigation now converged on Mr. and Mrs. Triton.

More information was clearly needed, and I needed to talk to Archer and Tavington. I just didn't know how to get both of them up to speed without revealing the existence of my Mysterious Friend. Archer would immediately question whether this person was behind last year's beatdown of Judge Yu during Annabelle's politically motivated murder trial. Tavington would be required to report suspected unethical behavior to the state bar and law enforcement.

Figuring out what to do with all this would require some careful thought tonight.

CHAPTER 5

"Who is Ryan Anderson?" I muttered to no one in particular as I sat in the study of our home in Prior Lake. It was just our luck that this particular surname was common in Minnesota, so searching for public information was like trying to find a needle in a haystack.

Frustrated, I pulled off my reading glasses and rubbed my tired eyes for a few moments. Setting the readers aside, I leaned back in my comfy leather chair and took a sip of one of the rare bourbons we had brought back from a recent trip to the Bourbon Trail in Kentucky with our old friends. I took my bourbon on the rocks with a clear ice cube because one of those old friends thought we shouldn't disrespect fine bourbon by diluting it with anything more than that. He was right. Sullying a small batch like this with soda would be tantamount to a crime against humanity.

It was late at night. Heidi had gone to bed a few hours ago just after Riley and Jeffrey had gotten Mary to bed. Now that the house was quiet, it was time to sit in the study and contemplate the situation for a bit. Today's visit to what turned out to be a speakeasy on steroids heralded the unsettled feeling that events might be spinning out of control. Again.

When things got out of control last year, Annabelle was charged with the Bimbo Bits murder of my cousin's mooching daughter.

The only other thing I had managed to accomplish this evening was creating a dossier about Mrs. Kettle. Turned out she was a very wealthy socialite and known acquaintance of Samantha Triton. They had hosted several public fundraisers together, so there was plenty of fawning press about their friendship and collaboration. The media always loved glamorous socialites who threw their money around. Despite all that press, absolutely none of it mentioned Ryan Anderson.

I hadn't closed down my laptop yet, so the popup announcing an email caught my eye. It was from Annabelle. She was still working and sent a couple of files over, so I opened the message.

> Dad, attached is an employee list of Triton Industries that Terry Triton sent today. Also attached is the HR file on Erik Johnson. So far Terry is following through in helping us look into his dad's jail sentence. Dakota Aerospace is Bill Harrison's conglomerate and Harrison is Martin Triton's longtime rival. — A

With no insights born of bourbon-inspired brilliance coming to mind, I opened the file for Erik Johnson. There wasn't a lot beyond the basics. Age. Hiring date. Date missing from work. No reprimands. Poached away from a managerial position in a unit of Dakota Aerospace, which was an intriguing connection but there wasn't any more context about that. Worked for Triton Industries in the finance department for 5 years. Promoted. Looked pretty much like an otherwise unremarkable dead end.

Opening the employee file next didn't look too promising, either. Thousands of names, listed next to their business units. Pages and pages of it.

"Well, shit," I muttered before taking another sip of caramel-colored bourbon and looking up at nothing in particular. Nothing like receiving useless data to make you decide to call it a day.

Before closing the laptop lid, I decided to search for "Anderson" in the employee list just to see what it returned. It was a whim. A last gasp to feel like I at least tried.

Ryan Anderson was listed as an employee of Triton Industries. And not just any employee. He is the security chief of Triton Industries. This man was responsible for protecting both the facilities and IT servers of the enterprise. I was suddenly wide awake, and it wasn't until the middle of the night before I took a break from researching the elusive Mr. Anderson.

* * *

A loud squeal of "Papa!" echoed through the house while I stomped around the top floor of Annabelle's place, pretending to loudly chase my granddaughter, Emily. With that girl, the thrill was in the chase, so I made sure only to catch her occasionally and usually let her barely escape by the skin of her teeth the other times. Once that happened, the "gotcha" roughhousing was brief before I'd release Emily back into the wild, only to begin the chasing anew. She had grown into a quick, mobile little six-year-old.

Soon, playtime was over and I had settled down in my spot in the living room with Archer and Annabelle. They were already on their second cups of coffee while I started on my first. By now, this had become the team's working routine when at Annabelle's place. The coffee was hot, dark and bitter. Its delicate, earthy aroma wafted up and promised motivation.

With a cup of it held to his nose, Archer breathed deeply before taking a sip. He never took his eyes from the computer screen while he enjoyed the brew. "Hmmmm," he grunted in satisfaction. Annabelle's slow-drip, pour-over coffee was among his favorite coffees.

Smiling, Annabelle's attention returned to her own laptop to gather her thoughts for a few moments as we worked. "I wasn't able to run down much more regarding the drive-by shooting in St. Paul. Seemed to be just another slaying between gangbangers and nothing more is bubbling up beyond learning the identity of the shooter. Other than the intel we received from Mrs. Jamans when she asked us to look into why her boy was killed in a drug deal, the only person who talked to us was a fan of the show who is in the rival gang and needs his identity protected," summarized Annabelle. "I'm thinking we report back to Mrs. Jamans on what we found and wrap up our investigation. There isn't enough for us here for us to do a show episode."

This was the kind of investigation outcome that Annabelle had the hardest time accepting. After her husband Brock was murdered by Zoe Finch several years ago, Annabelle had finally learned to cope with his absence with the help of her family. It was never easy, and she's routinely confronted by terrible evidence of violence impacting families that "Murder in Minnesota" kept uncovering.

Annabelle had initially started the show to highlight the unjust sentences given to criminals in Minnesota, like the slap on the wrist given to Zoe for killing Brock, and the show had steadily grown into an investigative force in the state that continually exposed the good and the bad of our justice system. The show's growth suddenly exploded last year when corrupt bureaucrats tried to disappear Annabelle with a fraudulent show trial. They tried to put their thumbs on the scales of justice just so they could get rid of her muckraking and public airing of their bad behavior.

Due to her highly public exoneration and the comeuppance of those duplicitous kleptocrats, the show had acquired a national profile that was widely popular. That exoneration had come at an additional price, one secretly paid by me. I was still paying, every time my new Mysterious Friend needed me to fix something.

Because of that recent history, Annabelle has an especially soft spot for grieving parents and spouses. She was one herself, and she had no qualms about sympathizing with her listeners and crime victims. That sympathy is on full display in the Jamans investigation, because Mrs. Jamans is a grieving mother whose child had been murdered, and all we could turn up was the possible name of her child's purported killer. Of course, we would turn that information over to Mrs. Jamans. It would be little consolation for her, and Annabelle's heart would hurt with the knowledge that we ultimately couldn't do much to help.

As a former detective, Archer has a tougher hide than Annabelle and he doesn't wear his heart on his sleeve. He is a man with the natural instinct to do what is right as best he can, yet underneath that armored exterior beats the heart of an experienced cynic who knows life is messy and usually involves shortcuts somewhere. Long divorced, Archer is the father of a grown son, Taylor, who lives in another part of the country. I suspect Archer sees Annabelle as his surrogate child while Taylor isn't nearby. Over the past year, she has become the daughter Archer never had, so now Annabelle essentially has two father figures in her life.

Nonverbal head nods indicated Annabelle should go ahead and deliver the paltry news to Mrs. Jamans. Archer had the most experience at delivering terrible news, but he could never match Annabelle's natural warmth and empathy as a mother who had experienced the trauma of loss.

Annabelle then turned to our biggest project. The Triton investigation. By now I had already brought the others up to speed about Ryan Anderson's identity.

"Do we know who was following us the other day?" she asked. Being tailed tends to get our attention.

Archer shook his head. "No. All we know is it was the Ghost of Erik Johnson behind the wheel, and a solid ID on the make and model of his black SUV."

"Any leads on how we solve this mystery?" she asked.

It had dawned on me that there was a way to investigate Ryan Anderson, and I was still slightly annoyed that I hadn't started earlier than last night. Maybe I was slipping in my old age. Whatever the issue was, once I finally started to get my act together it was back to the same methods of analyzing a complex, fact-based problem that I had used during my career in corporate litigation.

That methodology involved making a case summary. Unlike the Constitution, my case summaries are living documents that are edited as a situation progresses. As known facts are learned, they are populated into a form that is divided into several sections that organize my thinking. There is a section for a short Summary of the overall case, followed by another section identifying the Players and their backgrounds. After that are an analysis of known Legal Issues and a Chronology, often called a Timeline. There are other sections that I add if it's litigation, like background of a judge and prior rulings for pertinent issues, but now that I'm retired I don't often use those kinds of sections.

My experience with case summaries often highlights a section that other people tend to think is of somewhat lesser importance that should be rolled into one of the other sections: Chronology. Harping on the importance of a Chronology sounds like I'm nerding-out, but a detailed Chronology typically displays the known facts right in front of your face in a simple way that really helps to expose fraud. It allows the reader to quickly identify how a scheme went down, and by exposing that data it also allows a careful reader to also deduce what is missing. The Known Unknowns, as it were.

Done well, a case summary is a powerful tool to guide a lawyer through every step in claims and litigation and enables a lawyer to initially identify how the final outcome of those processes was likely to come about. Knowing the end game at the beginning is a huge advantage over those lawyers or parties who hadn't figured out how to get there before the procedural festivities began.

With all that background experience in mind, the draft case summary I had begun cobbling together last night about Ryan Anderson helped clarify the overarching situation in my head. The high-level summary is that as the corporation's security chief, Anderson would know where a lot of the skeletons are hidden in the company's closets. He's also compromised by his secret love triangle with the client's spouse, a facet of this mess the rest of the MiM team is currently unaware of.

This is where Chronology starts to show its worth. Drug-induced sex tigress Tammy Kettle and Samantha Triton were bumping uglies with Anderson before Martin Triton became a permanent resident of Minnesota's penal system. Erik Johnson was also an employee, and his corpse was found floating in Lake Minnetonka a couple months ago. Johnson was poached from the rival company whose owner Martin was convicted of murdering. This is all stuff I know as of today. It's the deeper details behind those events that were missing.

As I had learned while getting to know Archer over cold beers the past year, both his and my experience about methods of finding the truth can be pretty similar. One preferred method to uncover secrets, fraud and deceit is to start pushing those buttons that the known and unknown facts suggest need pushing. Reactions tend to bring the truth to light.

Once I had put it all into the Chronology, I sipped my drink and couldn't help but notice what we didn't know since it was now right in front of my face. I normally wouldn't factor Johnson into this case summary except that his SUV was spotted tailing us after we left Samantha Triton's place mere days ago. That was enough of a connection to include him for now. The initial Known Unknowns that required looking into include whether there is more of a connection between Johnson and Anderson than merely being employed by the same large employer. Other Known Unknowns required exploring the relationship triangle of Anderson, Kettle and Triton. The final Known Unknown that I saw pertained to Johnson's SUV. We needed to know the story behind that SUV, who was driving it, and why we had been tailed.

Pushing buttons typically needs to be done purposefully, with some planning. Pushing buttons randomly, like how I pack the truck of a car (similar to a raccoon on meth), leads you to the GIGO principle. Garbage In Garbage Out. Better to be deliberate about which particular buttons you believe will achieve the goal. This is true whether you're just trying to aggravate your annoying sibling or just to cause an opposing player to make a mistake. Do it well, and you end up living rent-free in someone's head and finding leverage over them to achieve the purpose you had in mind.

Right now, the goal is to find out more information to help us determine if someone is hiding something. Based on what we know right now, Anderson seems to have ties to both Samantha Triton and Johnson. The buttons to push will be his weak spots that give us leverage.

Refocusing on the present, I saw Archer shrug in response to Annabelle's question about leads. Now was the time to throw in my two cents.

"I'd like to talk with Ryan Anderson, the Security Chief of Triton Industries." My statement was met with confused expressions on the faces of Annabelle and Archer.

"To get more information on Johnson?" asked Archer.

I nodded. "Yup. See what he can dig up for us. Terry Triton authorized access to anybody and any resource, I'd like to start at the top and see if anything resonates." Even without revealing what I know to Annabelle and Archer, reaching out to Anderson under the guise of his security position with the company was an approach that still made some sense in its own right.

Annabelle and Archer nodded in agreement now, so it was easy to get them to go along with this. It turned out that getting time with Ryan Anderson took longer to arrange than it should have.

* * *

Archer glanced at me from the driver's seat while we drove north on Highway 169 towards Minnetonka for our meeting with Ryan Anderson. It was one of those bright, sunny mornings that often occur after a cold weather front rolls through. Everything looked and smelled fresh and clean after the powerful thunderstorms of the prior evening, which stood in stark contrast to our discussion in the car.

"Mr. Anderson's been dodging us," Archer said matter-of-factly. "Seven rescheduling messages and a missed meeting with a crappy excuse for why establishes that he is trying to avoid us." During his career, Archer had seen just about every possible bob and weave by detainees trying to avoid taking punches in a police interview. The man was no stranger to elusive behavior.

I snorted and nodded. "Yeah. Terry Triton had to make him make time for us. The 'busy security executive' dodge wasn't going to work forever. Dude's got something to hide."

Turning his head, Archer suddenly focused on my conclusion. "Like what?"

Shaking my head, I said, "I dunno. Not yet anyway. But my red flags are waving because something doesn't feel right. Not sure what it is."

"Welcome to the club. We'll play it by ear and see how this meeting goes down," Archer said.

Twenty minutes later, we were ushered into Ryan Anderson's office. Without rising from his desk, which had nothing on it other than a laptop PC, Anderson motioned for us to sit in the chairs opposite him. Although he was sitting, it was apparent Anderson was a tall man with a slender physique. Blonde with brown eyes, he had a piercing stare that seemed practiced and deliberate.

"So sorry for the delays in getting together with you gentlemen. I'm a bit pressed for time, so what can I do for you?" Anderson said in a deep bass voice in a way that clearly communicated he wasn't sorry and was slightly miffed at being forced to squeeze us into his busy schedule.

Archer kept his Game Face in place and started first. "Thank you for taking the time, Mr. Anderson. As you've been advised, we've been asked to look into the conviction of Mr. Triton ..." he began saying when Anderson interrupted him.

"I know that. What is it you want from me?" Anderson said brusquely.

Nonplussed, Archer simply said, "Access."

"To what?" Anderson asked curtly.

Raising an eyebrow, Archer coldly said, "To your network files pertaining to Erik Johnson."

Without missing a beat, Anderson screwed his face into a look of confusion and he half muttered, "Who the hell is Erik Johnson?"

Archer pressed on. "The employee whose corpse was found floating in Lake Minnetonka." Archer knew Triton Industries had already had to search its networked files regarding Johnson as part of the original investigation into his death. Jogging Anderson's memory of that effort shouldn't be too difficult for Archer.

Eyebrows raising slightly in surprise, Anderson quickly regained his footing. "Oh, THAT guy. Been awhile since his name came up. Yeah, sure. I can get you those records." He turned towards his laptop PC that had been pushed aside when we entered the room, and typed a few commands without telling us what he was doing. "Mmmm. Looks like we have north of 22,000 records. You want I should see if we have any security footage of him as well?"

Nodding, I finally spoke. "Yes, please. Especially for the week of his disappearance, coinciding with those times your systems recorded him badging in and out of work."

Since Anderson had responded as though he didn't recognize the name Erik Johnson, Archer and I figured it would be unproductive to directly ask Anderson about his interactions with Johnson. It could only be one of two types of feedback that we would get now. Anderson would affirm he was unfamiliar with Johnson either because he truly didn't know Johnson, or because he was lying. Either way would yield more of the same from Anderson and we wouldn't learn anything that we didn't already know.

"Yes, I can run down our video feeds and include that information for you, Mr. Finch. Was there anything else you two needed?"

As Archer and I traded glances to see if the other had something else, a man in his early 30s knocked and entered without waiting for Anderson's response.

"Here's a stick with those records you just requested," said the man as he walked in and held out a memory stick. Anderson waved it off and lazily pointed towards me. "It's for them, Mike. Thanks for the quick turnaround."

Archer only had a few small questions regarding what we were looking to accomplish with Mr. Anderson. While I listened to Archer professionally question Anderson, I noticed Archer was less interested in *what* Anderson said than in *how* Anderson said it. Anderson was vague and trying to mask his evasiveness behind a veneer of busy professionalism. As Archer probed a bit further into the investigative steps taken by Anderson's department in response to the original investigation of Johnson, Anderson shrugged off answering definitively and blamed his lack of specific memory on being overwhelmed with work.

Once we were back in the car, both of us were alone with our thoughts as we drove through Minnetonka in sunny, mid-day weather. It had remained nice and comfortable outside during our brief meeting with Mr. Anderson, although now a slight breeze had picked up. Neither of us paid any attention as we were lost in our thoughts. The quiet in the car only lasted for five miles before Archer broke it.

"I hate being lied to." Archer's statement was simple, yet said so much.

Snorting, I nodded in agreement. "Anderson lied his ass off. Proving it is going to be the hard part."

Nodding towards the memory stick I had dropped into the cup holder between the front seats, Archer asked, "You want to do the honors or should I?"

I pulled the laptop PC from the backpack sitting on the backseat and booted it up. Soon I was scrolling through a seemingly endless list of records while we drove back to Prior Lake.

Archer glanced at my rapid scrolling and deduced what I was doing. "Even you can't speed-read that fast. Doing some pattern recognition instead?"

I half-smiled in a cunning way. "Yep. Five bucks says you won't guess what I see already."

"None of Anderson's private records about Johnson?" Archer definitely took that bet.

"Correct in one. Bastard tried to bury that omission by flooding us with tons of other records. Good thing we were expecting that," I said without looking up, despite my tendency to get carsick if I read more than a few pages while sitting in a moving vehicle. Weirdly, I never got car sick if I was the driver, only if sitting in the back seat or reading in a vehicle. I also hated getting car sick.

Both of us suspected Anderson will be too clever by half in his records deliveries by excluding his own notes and so on from those deliverables. Noticing that Anderson's own records are missing will cause us to begin to focus on Anderson.

"How do we deal with that?" Archer asked rhetorically. We had worked together long enough to know each other knew what to do already, so the question had become somewhat of a joke between us.

"We push buttons!" I said, like a student who happened across the right answer. I pulled my phone and did just that by pushing the button to call Terry Triton. He answered in two rings and I put my phone on speaker so Archer could listen in.

"Mr. Finch, any progress?" Triton said in lieu of a more conventional answer greeting like, "Hello?" or "This is Terry Triton."

"Mr. Triton—" I began when he interrupted.

"Call me Terry, please," he interjected.

"OK. Terry, we obtained some records from Mr. Anderson's office pertaining to Mr. Johnson, but I'm afraid we've encountered some unexpected hiccups."

"Anything I can help with?" Terry asked.

I half-smiled even though Terry couldn't see my expression. "I think so. It seems we only obtained partial network records pertaining to Mr. Johnson from the company. I'm sure it was just an oversight because he's so busy, but we don't have any of Mr. Anderson's own records pertaining to Mr. Johnson. Could you have someone on your staff get those for us? I don't want to bother someone as busy as Mr. Anderson again."

"You'll have them in hand by the end of the week. I'll have my personal secretary call you to make arrangements shortly."

"Thank you, Terry. We really appreciate the assistance." I said this in my most sincere sounding voice.

"Gentlemen, let me say again, anything you need, just call me on my company cell phone. You have no idea how much I appreciate your help in looking through everything."

Terry terminated the call and I exchanged glances with Archer.

"He sounded annoyed, but not at you," Archer surmised. "You think this will push Anderson's buttons? Terry's secretary isn't even going to give Anderson a head's up about scraping together his own records."

"I'm counting on it. Every security chief who is worth a shit will have his own 'bots in the system to give them a heads up that their own personal drive has been accessed by someone else and what data was copied. *That's* the button I'm counting on being pushed." Both my words and the tone in which I said them were cold.

Eyebrow rising, Archer asked, "What if Anderson isn't as paranoid as you're hoping?"

"He will be. That man has something to hide," I said confidently. Archer just didn't know that I expected to find more connections in the data we were going to receive.

CHAPTER 6

ARCHER RESIDENCE "THE SWAMP" — PRIOR LAKE

"Anderson tried to hide his records relating to Johnson? Does he think we're stupid?" summarized Annabelle in an indignant tone. She was pretty annoyed at what would ordinarily be an obvious attempt to deceive us.

I barked a small laugh at the same time that Archer snorted slightly before taking a sip of his steaming mug of coffee. We were sitting in the sunroom at Archer's home, one of four homes overlooking a small, reedy pond in Prior Lake, while we sipped fresh mugs of coffee and watched the rain fall from gray, overcast skies. The pond was so small, it had no name other than the informal one Archer had tagged both the pond and his home with. When we gathered at "The Swamp," it always meant at Archer's place.

"Best part is Anderson thought his data was walled off and encrypted from prying eyes but forgot the Board of Directors has override access to everything," Archer noted. He loved exposing bad actors who thought they were being clever. While Anderson thought he was safe behind his homebrewed firewalls and encryption, he just hadn't expected Terry's trusted secretary would use Terry's own director level credentials to search for records.

Archer and I had been working on the records from Terry for the better part of a week. There were thousands of electronic documents, mostly instant messaging that had been auto-saved by Anderson's own 'bots instead of being deleted immediately like ordinary instant messages. Anderson's cleverness was going to hoist the man by his own petard and those messages might blow open a hole in this investigation.

"Anderson's messaging with 'S' possibly links him to Johnson's murder. We just aren't ready to run a story on air because there are far too many unknowns. We don't know the identity of 'S', the reason why Anderson or someone else ended Johnson, the identity of our mysterious tail and so on. Plus, we don't know if any of that helps Martin because he was convicted for killing Harrison, not Johnson. I spoke with Terry and he's agreed not to expose Anderson yet as a favor to us so we can keep digging," I summarized succinctly. I could see that we had begun to crack open this matter, but for now it seems like we have a two-tracked investigation and we're only making progress on the track we actually hadn't been hired to look into. So far that meant it was Johnson 1, Harrison 0.

Annabelle, looking tired because Emily's swim meet ran long last night, nodded thoughtfully. "We need to focus on finding links between Johnson and Harrison. I got a gut feeling these deaths are linked by something closer than coincidence."

Archer's eyebrow rose as he asked, "What if we still don't have all the records?"

Given the size of the enterprise, my experience already told me it was nearly certain we didn't get all the records. There are too many possible data streams from too many devices, which was always bothersome for the phase of litigation called Discovery. Something about this line of thought jogged my memory and then it hit me.

"Company cell phones!" I exclaimed without first giving the others the context of what I had been thinking.

"So?" Archer responded. "We don't have any lines bugged, and landlines aren't much of a thing nowadays."

I shook my head. "No, remember Terry said for us to call him on his company cell phone the other day? He had no landline in his office," I said.

"And? We're not looking into Terry," Archer remarked.

"Anderson's desk and table likewise lacked a landline when we visited," I pointed out. "Presumably the head of security for a large company has either a company cell phone or their cell bill is paid for by the company because of the number of calls he would receive."

Archer's eyes suddenly widened in comprehension. "Company cell phones," he said, completing the thought. "But if it's an SMS text, the cellular provider typically only retains those for a couple months."

"Unless their company phones are subject to a litigation hold because there's a Discovery order that might encompass cell phone records," I noted. "And most large companies have litigation holds going most of the time."

"Call Terry and see if he can get us those records," Archer said. "For both Johnson and Anderson."

* * *

A few days later we met again at The Swamp. It was just past sunset, and the pink–and-purple-hued sky framed the trees over the pond. Archer poured bourbon several fingers deep over ice and handed me a glass.

"Jackpot-ish," Archer commented after taking a sip and grunting slightly in satisfaction.

"The bourbon?" I asked.

Snorting, Archer said, "Well, that too. Turns out you were right about Anderson's phone records being held under a long-term hold for litigation with the company attorneys."

I half-smiled smugly. "I'll bet it hurt a lot to say that."

While the text messages had been held, it still took more digging because they didn't contain much. What was more important was that a true copy digital image of the phone's entire contents had been made for litigation. That copy contained all the apps that were on the phone, along with the passwords for those apps. We found a private messaging app that would not have revealed its secrets were it not for the fact that Anderson hadn't changed his password for the app since the point in time where the phone's image had been copied. We had been able to bootstrap the phone's copied password access that had been provided to us by the company lawyers in the form of a copied digital image, and we got into the app that way. That's where the data goldmine had been downloaded from.

Archer chuckled. "More than you can ever imagine," he joked. He clinked bourbon glasses with me and we both took another sip. "So now we know 'S' is Samantha Triton and that Anderson was bumping uglies with her and another gal by the name of Tammy Kettle. We also know that he wasn't too bright because he was using a company cell phone while it was still subject to litigation discovery so all those data records got swept up."

"Unfortunately, all the new data does is provide some context. But not much more," I said slowly, eyes taking in the fading colors of the sky while we sat in the recliners in his sunroom. Neither of us said anything while we pondered and sipped bourbon. Finally, I asked Archer a question. "Anderson doesn't know about the records the cell company turned over, does he?"

Shaking his head, he said, "Not that I could tell. I bet he forgot all about that app link he sent to a third-party app from his phone with the app store software restrictions jail broken."

"And those messages we now have vaguely mentioned a "J" a couple times without identifying who that was. Based on the records containing corresponding dates and actions, it's not too difficult to identify J as Erik Johnson."

Now it was Archer's turn to nod. "Yeah. We know who he is, and that the messaging doesn't clearly state anyone is the culprit in Johnson's death. They were at least smart enough to avoid stupidly putting anything too damning in writing."

It seemed as if we had reached an impasse. We had learned a few identities and connections between the players, but we were still lacking a picture of the complete game they were playing.

"Time to push a few more buttons and see what happens?" I asked.

Archer smiled conspiratorially. "Oh yeah. I'm thinking we meet Mr. Anderson again. Get his perspective on the new records."

I chuckled. "Like you read my mind."

Archer fixed me with a mock, horrified expression. "I try to avoid dark places like that. Scares me."

CHAPTER 7

"Your message said you acquired some additional records you wanted to discuss?" Anderson said, leaning back in his seat at his desk.

His voice conveyed both concern and confusion about which records we had mentioned in our message. Archer and I knew better than to provide Anderson with advance notice of the exact records we were going to discuss. We were there to watch his reaction.

Wordlessly, Archer slid printed copies of what we were referring to across the desk. Anderson picked them up and looked intently at the cover page for a few moments. When he turned the first page, his eyes widened in horror.

"As you can see, yellow highlighted text beginning on the second page reveals a sexual relationship between you, a Mrs. Tammy Kettle, and Mrs. Samantha Triton. Lots of graphic sexting between this triangle, don't you think?" Archer said gently, like he was breaking bad sports news to Anderson.

"What! How?" Anderson sputtered. He didn't get enough time to form anything more coherent before he was interrupted.

"Wanna tell us again about Erik Johnson?" I asked, my voice now a deep rasp.

Anderson's head tilted back in exasperation as he sighed and slumped his shoulders slightly in defeat. He took a few moments to process the possible consequences before responding.

Eyes leveled at me, Anderson said, "Martin Triton suspected Johnson was a spy working for Bill Harrison in some long running game of corporate espionage between Triton and Harrison. They were rivals most of their lives." Anderson's face communicated that he believed we didn't know anything about the two men's rivalry.

"The existence of their rivalry was pretty well publicized during Martin's murder trial. Can you tell us more?" I asked in an effort to keep Anderson talking.

Anderson sat more upright in his chair, put his elbows on his desk and crossed his arms for a moment while he mentally composed what he was going to say. "Martin asked me to investigate Johnson. I was able to determine that he was secretly still in the employ of Harrison and was tasked with stealing confidential financial data from Triton Industries that would give Dakota Aerospace a competitive advantage in some upcoming defense contracting bidding. Using the stolen information would have enabled Dakota Aerospace to shadow price Triton Industries while under-bidding slightly to make the Dakota Aerospace bid more competitive." "Why wouldn't Martin's company just adjust their bid? They could easily stay ahead of the competition then," Archer asked.

"Because bids don't become publicly available until after the winning bid is accepted. Only then can competitors look over each other's bids to see who won the contract and why," Anderson said. "Only thing that can happen after that is for losing competitors to try to find something to support a bid protest to try to reverse the awarding of the contract."

Archer nodded slightly in understanding. "So, Martin had Johnson eliminated to prevent being underbid by Harrison."

Anderson half-smiled, but there wasn't humor in it. "Actually, no. Martin directed me to turn Johnson to our side and feed Harrison false data."

"How did you manage that?" Archer asked. He was intrigued now.

"By offering triple what Harrison was paying him, and to provide a share of the revenues. It was a multi-billion-dollar contract, but that somehow wasn't enough for Johnson. So Martin had Samantha seduce Johnson to finally win him over."

Surprised and impressed by that level of ruthlessness, I was also somewhat confused. "So who killed Johnson? Was it a retaliation killing by Harrison or Martin?"

Anderson slowly shook his head, looking thoughtful now. "Actually, I don't think it was either of them. As far as I'm aware, Harrison didn't know we had turned Johnson. That made Johnson extremely useful to Martin in the long term by keeping Harrison down in the bidding wars. Same goes for me, since Johnson's new role made my own small ownership share of the company significantly more valuable with each contract that we won."

That was a plausible sounding and exculpatory, partial explanation, but it didn't actually answer my question. "OK. So, who do you *think* killed Johnson?" I probed further, emphasizing *think* to get Anderson's theory out into the open.

Anderson sighed and leaned back in his chair once again. "I *think*," he said, emphasizing the same word, "the answer might have something to do with Tammy. How? I dunno. Why? Also don't know. Just a gut feeling here, which is all I have left to offer."

Well, Anderson was wrong about that. Archer immediately asked, "So how did you and Samantha become involved?"

Anderson's eyebrows shot up. Clearly, he'd been hoping not to be asked that particular question. To his credit, he gave us a straight sounding answer. "Sam told me she was feeling low about being used by her husband to seduce Johnson. I guess she turned to me for comfort. As you can see, I'm single and Sam's both beautiful and wealthy. And before you ask, because I can see Mr. Archer getting ready to inquire, Sam introduced me to Tammy, whom she had been sexually involved with for years. We became involved all around."

"Why the gut feeling about Tammy?" I asked. "She say or do something?"

Anderson chuffed softly. His eyes were now unfocused somewhere on his desk. "She's a pretty jealous type of woman. Took her awhile to accept that Sam wanted to include me in their trysts. It took months for her to accept that loss of exclusivity, despite discovering her love of threesomes. Which also doesn't completely make sense because those two weren't exclusive to begin with, since both of them are married to different men." Anderson's eyes focused on me for a moment and he foresaw the question that I was about to ask.

"I suspect Sam let it slip to Tammy that Sam was separately banging Erik Johnson as a way to keep Johnson under her influence. Despite the, uh, dutiful aspect of it, Sam still seemed to enjoy sleeping with John-son. Tammy found out because she wanted an explanation why Sam was secretly disappearing for a couple hours here and there, taking away from Tammy's playtime with me and Sam," Anderson said. "That's why I have a gut feeling the answer has something to do with Tammy. But do I have direct evidence? No, and those records you printed are consistent with that."

The drive following our get-together with Mr. Anderson was quiet for the first ten minutes while we each processed what we had learned. We were on our way to meet Annabelle for lunch at El Burro Azul. Today the food truck was parked in the parking lot of a local chain of home goods store that Paul, the truck owner, had a good working relationship with.

Annabelle was already standing in line and waiting for our orders to come up. She knew Archer preferred the spicy chicken burrito, and I liked the hot street tacos. Minutes later, we were standing near the rear of my pickup truck and using the lowered tailgate as a makeshift table.

"Well? How did Anderson take the news?" Annabelle asked between bites.

"He rolled. Filled us in on a conspiracy surrounding Johnson's corporate espionage for Bill Harrison and how Martin turned him into a double agent. Anderson also gave us his perspective on who he thinks offed Johnson. Problem is, he is guessing based on what he thinks is the motive, which is Samantha using sex to finally gain control over Johnson with Martin's blessing and that possibly not going over too well with Tammy Kettle, who is Samantha's secret lesbian lover. Jacob and I think he was being pretty truthful with us and none of that whole story conflicts with the records we found," I summarized succinctly.

Eyes wide, Annabelle swallowed her food while she digested what I had just said. "Holy shit!" she finally managed to sputter. Then her blue eyes narrowed and she brushed a lock of red hair away from her face. "So, what do we do now?"

Archer chuffed. "That's the million-dollar question, isn't it?"

Annabelle said, "We need to find something to drive a wedge between Tammy and Samantha. Get someone to talk."

My burner phone beeped with an incoming message that I read. Shocked, I read it twice. Suddenly, I smiled evilly. "I have an idea."

Annabelle looked at me. "What?"

"I have a friend who might be able to help us do that," I said.

Archer rolled his eyes. "Your friends are the kind who get us into trouble."

I barked a laugh. "Oh, they excel at that."

* * *

"Solid Waste, Inc.?" Archer said as he read the sign on the outer wall of the ratty old warehouse that was barely legible in the weak light cast by the sconce above the sign. "This is your big idea?" It was dark, several hours past midnight. It was that time of night when it would be smarter for guys like us to be elsewhere.

I didn't look up from an app I was checking on my burner phone so Archer got no response other than me opening the decrepit entrance and walking into a small, dimly lit, filthy waiting room. In the window that appeared to be a former ticket booth window was the same unfriendly looking face. My new buddy, Bruno, watched us with suspicion until we approached close enough for him to recognize me.

To my surprise, Bruno's roughhewn face suddenly lit up in a broad smile. "Ah, welcome back, Mr. Fancypants. I'll let Mr. Sorvino know you're here." Then he disappeared through the back door and we were alone.

"Welcome back? What the hell kind of friends do you have here, Dante?" Archer whispered to me worriedly.

I whispered back. "The kind in low places."

Archer never got a chance to say more. The security door suddenly opened and in walked Tony Sorvino, wearing a well-tailored black suit with subtle pinstriping, a red tie with a gold collar bar, and black leather dress shoes. Except for the gaudy gold rings on his fingers and gold watch, he would have looked completely out of place in this dumpy warehouse.

"I didn't see any drones from the feds out there. I assume they didn't find the speakeasy last time?" I asked, handing a manila envelope to Sorvino.

Sorvino pulled out the document from the envelope and squinted as he read the first sentence. "Many thanks, my friend! Everything is as you requested. If you and your ex-cop friend here will follow me, we can get started," Sorvino said jovially as he shook our hands. "I believe you know the way." We walked through the security door into the near darkness beyond.

Sorvino then answered me. "You are correct. They made it through the security door as we expected them to, but they never found the entrance. Just a back exit and abandoned equipment and some hallway connections to adjacent buildings. My sources said they thought you simply disappeared into another building, and they are busy looking elsewhere thanks to your idea. Very clever, that idea," Sorvino said as we began descending into the building's netherworld. Neither Sorvino nor myself explained to Archer what my idea had been.

The richly decorated entertaining space of the underground speakeasy was busy at this time of night. Some sort of seductive music greeted us along with drunks standing at the bar along a backlit wall that highlighted an excellent selection of liquor. Archer was wisely keeping quiet, but when I chanced a glance at him, the incredulous look he shot at me spoke volumes. Archer's attention returned to appraise the crowd in the dimly lit room for a few moments while Sorvino grinned broadly at Archer's reaction.

"Hedonism, I think you call it. I call it being a good proprietor," Sorvino said. "Pleasure. Pain if you want it. Companionship. Drugs. Booze. Influence. Everything you could want or need."

The room was filled with all manner of "hedonism." Men and women in various stages of undress. Visible chains and leathers. Bare skin. Orgy-like acts with participants and voyeurs. Nude dancers. Sweat, syringes, coke and bourbon made for an overwhelming olfactory experience accentuated by the poor lighting that limited viewing to glimpses of ongoing sins.

I chuffed and smirked slightly. "Good party," I said, impressed with the scale of festivities I could see.

Gesturing with his hand, Sorvino smiled more broadly and simply said, "This way, gentlemen."

We followed him down one of the connecting hallways and entered a room with a glass wall and several comfortable-looking chairs facing the glass. Plainly visible a few feet away through the glass was a threesome, two very young "men" and a beautiful blonde in her upper 50s.

"Might as well get comfortable and enjoy the show. She'll be a while," I said to Archer. Sorvino joined us in the chairs while we passed the time.

"Who are they?" Archer asked without looking away from the entertainment. He wasn't clear on why we were here because I hadn't told him anything other than there was a way of pushing some more buttons for our investigation and that he wouldn't like it.

Pointing with a tilt of my head, I said, "That rather enthusiastic lady is Tammy Kettle."

Archer's head snapped over to stare hard at me before returning his attention to the show. He motioned to me and muttered in my ear, "We need to communicate more."

He hadn't seen a picture of Mrs. Kettle before, and my answer was about the last thing he had expected to hear. I knew Archer well enough now to know it takes a lot to shock him, but since he had not been on a Vice Squad in a long time, the last 20 minutes weren't what he was used to encountering at work.

Mrs. Kettle and her energetic young male friends eventually finished having their fun and they began dressing. As she was pulling up her skimpy black lace panties, she looked up and waved at us with a smile because the glass wasn't a two-way mirror. It was just glass and she knew we had watched the show. Minutes later, she joined us in our lounge.

"Oh, I hope you're here to join me this time. You and your handsome friend," Mrs. Kettle said as she hugged me. The drugged redness around her eyes once again made her blue eyes appear even brighter.

"Mrs. Kettle, we're on the job again. Need to ask you a few questions," I said gently. Picking up on my continued standoffish behavior, Mrs. Kettle withdrew from hugging me. Archer simply stood to the side with his arms crossed while he waited for us to proceed.

"What is it?" she asked. Both Archer and I could see she was stoned out of her mind on something, but she retained enough awareness to still be responsive to questioning.

"Erik Johnson," I said.

High as she was, Mrs. Kettle recoiled in horror. "I didn't kill Erik!" she hissed.

It was the answer Archer and I had expected, so I hit her with the follow-up question. "OK. Then who did?"

"Why would I know that?" Mrs. Kettle sat down and began pulling on her shoes in what she imagined to be a message to us that we were dismissed.

"We have complete copies of the messages exchanged between your love triangle with Ryan and Samantha. Wanna tell us again about Erik

Johnson?" I said. My deep voice was already starting to sound a bit raspy and threatening.

Mrs. Kettle's head snapped up to stare hard at me. Her glare was broken moments later by Archer holding up a small sheaf of paper with portions of yellow highlights on it. It was another copy of the printed messaging we had broken Anderson with earlier.

Her surprised look suddenly turned into a sneer. "So what? My husband knows all about the three of us."

I realized Mrs. Kettle must have been thinking we intended to blackmail her by threatening to expose her to her husband because he was a prominent plastic surgeon in the west metro. Perhaps her thoughts were limited by her intoxicated state. She just wasn't thinking big enough.

I half-smiled and tilted my head slightly to the left for a moment. "Mrs. Kettle, we really don't care about your marriage relationship. What we *do* care about is justice. Justice for the dead, and the wrongly incarcerated. And that's where you come in," I said as I watched her reactions. She wasn't buying it, so I continued. "We're not the police. Not even him, anymore," I said with a hook of my thumb over my right shoulder at Archer. "We're investigators for 'Murder in Minnesota.' We find out what really happened as best we can, and we present the evidence online for several million weekly listeners."

Mrs. Kettle shrugged noncommittally now. Her reactions were still "off" due to whatever drugs she had ingested. "So you embarrass me with some harmless fun? A couple middle-aged guys like you yapping about threesomes on a podcast will just raise my profile in the gossip news pieces ..." she was saying when I cut her off.

"And our video of you fucking two rather young men. Boys, really," I said calmly, dropping the f-bomb for emphasis. "That tends to be graphic and changes how you will be spoken of by the chattering class instead of them merely gossiping about it."

"Grainy phone video? Who cares?" she retorted.

Sorvino spoke up. "Actually, it's 4k video. Four very high-quality cameras. Excellent coverage from all angles."

Mrs. Kettle's face turned into an indignant mask of rage. "How dare you! You can't do …" she began to rant. This time Sorvino cut her off.

"You failed to pay your tab for the last couple visits, Mrs. Kettle. You owe me $100,000 for services rendered and it's time to settle up."

The shock on Mrs. Kettle's face was priceless. She just hadn't considered that an entrepreneurial business proprietor like Tony Sorvino would be sure to collect the money he is owed. Sleeping with him a couple times never changed that, as Tony had pointed out to me when he and I privately discussed how tonight should go down. Especially since he had a well-stocked stable of easy women to bed any night he chose. In Sorvino's world, sex was cheap and sex with a beautiful, rich socialite was still just as cheap.

Tammy slowly realized she had been neatly boxed in. All we wanted was information or a confession, and all she had to do was tell us the truth or face a wave of public scorn and potential prosecution for getting stoned and screwing young men in a shady speakeasy. She sighed and her shoulders slumped slightly in defeat. "What do you want to know about Erik?"

"How was he killed?" Archer asked.

"Look, I'm not real sure, OK? Sam was sleeping with the guy to keep control over him. Then he threatened to go public with something if she didn't turn over her company shares to him. And then, he was just gone. It was like he never was, until his remains were found in Lake Minnetonka a while later. Only thing Sam said about him after he disappeared was that he left us using the Socratic Method. I have no idea what that even means."

Archer and I traded somewhat confused glances at her confession. Even Sorvino looked confused as to what it might mean. Judging from Mrs. Kettle's bewilderment, we certainly weren't going to learn anything more from her. She was an empty vessel, bereft of knowledge and soul.

I looked at Sorvino. "Tony, we're done here. I leave her to your tender mercies."

Sorvino nodded, no emotion at all visible on his face. "Take the hidden door out. You know the way."

Once we were back up on the streets, Archer looked around to get his bearings. It was still pitch dark. "Where are we?" he asked.

"A few blocks over from whence we came," I answered theatrically without bothering to look at him. We both were busy looking around in every direction while we made our way back to my truck. Encountering anyone out here at this time of night wasn't likely to lead to anything good. Soon we were in my black pickup truck, headed west on I-394 away from the warehouse district near downtown Minneapolis.

Archer had been scrutinizing the sparse traffic behind us for a while before he suddenly said, "No tails. Alright, spill it. You've met her before. And been to that place before. Time to lay your cards down."

"Recently, in fact. I was delivering a message down there a couple weeks back to our buddy, Mr. Sorvino, on behalf of a client of sorts. What got me past Bruno the gatekeeper and into their little den of iniquity was that I came bearing the gift of information about drone surveillance by the feds. Bruno …" I was saying when Archer interrupted.

"Was he the guy at the front entrance?"

Nodding, I continued. "Yeah. I don't know if that's his real name, it's just what I dubbed him in my head because it seems to fit. Anyway, Bruno hauls out a shotgun and blows the surveillance drone out of the sky. Then they ran a scramble drill down into the speakeasy and out the way you and I just exited. Only that time, Sorvino asked me to do him a solid and drive Mrs. Kettle home as she was finishing up with another pair of robust lads. True gentlemen that I am, I obligingly dropped her off at her mansion and declined her romantic advances." I chanced a glance at Archer when I finished speaking.

Archer couldn't have worn a more dubious expression had he tried.

"You really expect me to believe any of that bullshit?" he asked. "People like that track down people like you."

"Yeah, actually I do," I said as I pulled into a darkened parking lot that was deserted. Pulling out my regular license plates from under the backseat, I handed one to Archer and said, "Grab the screwdrivers and help me swap these back onto the truck. There's no security cameras here." To his credit, Archer didn't ask questions as we replaced the license plates. I guess he figured, rightly, this had been a sensible precaution to take for tonight's outing.

We were quiet until we turned south on Highway 169 towards Prior Lake, then I continued filling him in. "While that previous adventure to the speakeasy was full of surprises, the biggest surprise happened when we reached Mrs. Kettle's place. She lives near Samantha Triton, and when we passed Triton's place Mrs. Kettle lustily suggested that Mrs. Triton and our buddy, Mr. Ryan Anderson, were a throuple. Like tonight, Tammy was stoned out of her mind, so I couldn't be sure how credible any of that was, but it still was enough to be worth looking into. As our investigation played out, it happened to be information that was substantiated by Anderson and the evidence we've dug up so far."

"What's going to happen with Mrs. Kettle? Why did you set her up?" Archer said.

"I, and you, didn't do anything meaningful except show up tonight at Mr. Sorvino's invitation to deliver his legal documents and we happened to see an epic party and a peepshow during the delivery. He set her up because he wants his money, and I had checked in with my client, who merely extended the invitation. Sorvino appreciates his friends, and is tough on his enemies. I'm sure he will reach some sort of understanding with Mrs. Kettle on settling her bill."

Blowing out a breath, Archer shook his head. "You really worry me sometimes. We could've gotten in a helluva lot of trouble by getting swept up in a sting down there."

"And eventually released, because we weren't committing any crimes and were both fulfilling my legal duties and we were even investigating a crime ourselves. Which brings us back full circle. We have a motive and suspect for Johnson's death, but still nothing regarding Harrison."

Archer nodded. "We're still just solving the wrong crime. What was in the envelope you handed Sorvino? Even just delivering messages can get us arrested…" he was saying when I interrupted.

"I was delivering Sorvino's Last Will and Testament," I said with a half-smile, tugging the edge of my mouth.

"This is no joke, Dante. We get caught in a place like that sometime, and the hammer will hit hard."

Eyebrows raised now, I glanced at Archer in the pre-dawn light that was starting to illuminate the highway. "I know that. Which is why we, *for real*, just delivered his Last Will and Testament along with two certified copies for safekeeping. Sorvino executed the Will yesterday at Tavington's office, and it was written by both me and Tavington. That's a real-life legal document we just delivered, which is why we were there. You and I did nothing illegal merely by being there to deliver some privileged mail in a place where wicked things might have been going down. At best the government can try to assert some charges in an effort to get you to testify that you accompanied one of the bad guy's attorneys to deliver his Will and happened to see some fun things going on, but you can't say for sure since you did not interact with anyone and simply watched the Tammy Kettle Show. Nor do you know who the rest of them even are. *Why* some of them were there isn't particularly difficult to extrapolate, but that's just supposition since you were a delivery boy who was merely passing through."

Voice positively dripping with skepticism, Archer asked, "You really believe prosecutors would have any difficulty brushing all that aside? Really?"

I shrugged. "Who knows what prosecutors are capable of? Last year's debacle in prosecuting Annabelle showed some of them aren't too bright. Same goes on the defense side. So, what are they capable of proving with our delivery? That Sorvino paid two attorneys to draft his will, and we personally delivered it to the man's place of business because he lacks a conventional mailbox or other type of mailing address. We don't run his business or have any input regarding it, but everyone is entitled to pay for legal services and we are entitled to deliver said services in a privileged manner to protect our client's rights of confidentiality at a time and place of convenience to our client. It's really that simple."

"You know, Dante. Sometimes working with you is like dancing with the devil."

I snorted with laughter. "Noted. I did say that you would hate that adventure. Now how do we go about solving the crime we were hired to solve?"

Archer smiled wanly. "We really need to find some more buttons to push."

With that statement, I thought Archer had perfectly summed up the spot we now found ourselves in. Out of ideas.

CHAPTER 8

"Dad, there's a black SUV following us! It has Erik Johnson's license plate. I think it's the same one that followed us after we visited Mrs. Triton," Annabelle said. She sounded panicked over the phone.

"Where are you?" I asked hurriedly. The sun was beginning to set in the cloudless sky and I was in my truck headed home on Highway 13.

"Southbound on Marschall Road. We just crossed over the border between Shakopee and Prior Lake."

"I'm not far from you. Keep going and stay in the middle of the road as long as you can. I'll meet you where Marschall and 13 meet," I said, pressing down on the accelerator. "I'm getting Archer on the call." I called Archer and brought him into the conference.

"I still haven't …" Archer began saying by way of answering the phone when I interrupted.

"Jacob, shut up and listen. Annabelle is on the line. There's a black SUV following her south on Marschall Road. I told her to meet at Highway 13 and Marschall and not to stop until she gets there."

Archer immediately started issuing orders. "Agreed. I'm eastbound on Spring Lake Road now and will try to intercept. Don't let this guy rattle you and keep going until we catch up."

I could hear the squeal of tires over the phone as Archer quickly switched directions. He was on the residential road bordering the north shore of Spring Lake, and I was on the highway along the south of the lake.

It was an eerie feeling driving like a madman with an open phone line while no one said anything. I was going nearly 100 mph and the lines of the highway were a blur illuminated by the dying sun. I concentrated on not getting into a wreck as I heedlessly passed traffic.

Within mere minutes I was passing the wetlands along the southwestern part of the lake near the triangular intersection of Marschall Road, Highway 13, and a small part of Highway 282. I could see Annabelle's dark green Audi coming to a halt at the stop sign on Marschall Road with a black SUV right on her bumper. Archer's SUV suddenly skidded to a stop close behind the black SUV. He had turned his vehicle sideways to block the road with his driver's door facing away from the black SUV. No other vehicles were in sight and we weren't near any buildings.

The driver of the black SUV froze halfway out of the door with the unexpected arrival of two additional vehicles. I had the road blocked in front of the SUV. Archer and I popped out of our rides and leaned across our vehicles with pistols pointed at the black SUV.

Before a word was said, the driver of the black SUV disappeared into the vehicle and hit the gas in an effort to escape around Annabelle's car and my truck. Since Annabelle and Emily were already ducking down inside their vehicle and weren't in the way, Archer opened fire with his 9mm semi-automatic pistol and put a few rounds into the liftgate and rear window. Following suit, I fired three hollow point rounds with an old school .357 magnum. The heavy-caliber pistol emitted a distinctively loud, low boom and a blinding muzzle flash. Heavier bullets traveling at significantly higher velocity than Archer's 9mm had the desired effect as the engine of the black SUV seized while my last round shattered the front windshield. The driver lost control and hit a ditch with a powerful impact, causing the airbag to deploy.

Archer and I approached the black SUV cautiously, pistols pointed at the unconscious driver. To our surprise, it was Ryan Anderson. Other than a fair amount of blood streaming down his forehead from a severe laceration caused by the shattered glass, Anderson looked unharmed.

"Didn't you feel the need to disable the vehicle instead of trying for a zombie head shot?" Archer said offhandedly while dragging Anderson's unconscious body from the vehicle.

Snorting because Archer had fired first, I helped drag Anderson to my truck. "Only thing I felt was recoil. The third round went high and blew out the windshield. First two disabled the engine."

Before we threw him into my backseat, Archer quickly cuffed Anderson's hands together. He was still out cold. "Leave his SUV and let's get the hell out of here. Send Annabelle and Emily home and we'll take him to The Swamp. We'll question him there," he said with a tilt of his head in the direction we were about to drive.

We were gone in seconds and left no fingerprints behind.

* * *

THE SWAMP – PRIOR LAKE

"Wakey-wakey," Archer growled as he splashed ice water in Anderson's face. The man sputtered awake only to find himself securely tied to a metal chair.

"You can't—" Anderson started to say when Archer interrupted.

"Oh, yes. We definitely can," Archer said with a smile that carried neither warmth nor humor.

"I have rights. You have to turn me over to the police!" Anderson cried.

"Is that so?" I remarked in a gravelly voice dripping with sarcasm that clearly said we don't. "And here I was in the mood to commit another hate crime because an asshole was following my daughter and granddaughter."

Anderson snorted in response. He wasn't buying what we were selling so far.

"Know what we found out?" Archer asked rhetorically. "That you were behind the killing of Erik Johnson."

Anderson sneered. "You think so, huh? You think that is gonna scare me? What do you want?"

Undeterred, Archer continued. "Motive. Knowledge. Opportunity. Conspiracy. I can live with all those but cross the line and follow the girls … I get upset." Archer's seething anger was hard to ignore now.

"Yeah—" Anderson began to retort when I interrupted.

"Taking you off the board and putting your corpse in an unmarked grave gets you out of our hair," I said. "Why don't you tell us why you were following them? Give us a reason not to make you go missing."

Anderson shrugged slightly. "Samantha asked me to find out where all of you lived."

"Why?" Archer demanded. Knowing Archer as I have come to know him, that particular tone of his voice wasn't something to be trifled with. He was in a dark place and willing to do dark things right now.

To his credit, Anderson had finally recognized Archer's mood and decided to play it straight. "Actually, all she said was that she wanted to send some decorative plants as a gift for Socrates. Seriously, that's all she said after telling me to take Johnson's car. It was parked in her garage, and that's where it seems to live. I have no idea if she has any sort of permission to keep the SUV or not, and I don't think I want to know. Telling me to take a dead guy's car to track down your addresses was already more than I wanted to know."

Learning Samantha had possession of Johnson's SUV was a big piece of the puzzle that had been vexing us for weeks. More importantly, Samantha making Anderson try to track us clearly gave us a good idea of who we needed to focus on. She seemed to be trying to hide something and we still had no idea what to make of her reference to Socrates.

I traded looks with Archer. We both understood the implications of what Anderson just revealed to us. We also both know we're still solving the wrong crime but now our gut feelings are telling us we need to figure out Johnson's death to help us understand Harrison's.

"We want a bigger prize," Archer said without further preamble.

Anderson knew the opening pitch of a possible deal when he heard one. "You have my attention."

"Earlier you told us you thought maybe Tammy ended Johnson. Tammy claims it was Samantha. We weren't hired to find out Johnson's fate because we're supposed to find out who killed Harrison. We think this mystery is worth solving, don't you?" Archer said.

"How?" Anderson breathed. He didn't see where we were going with this.

"You confront Samantha. Tell her we've found partial information suggesting she is linked to both Johnson's death and Harrison's. We'll be there to record it and see how Samantha reacts. In exchange, we'll leave you alone if you continue to cooperate. If you don't ..." I said, leaving the sentence hanging to feed Anderson's imagination.

"She'll feed me to the fishes," said Anderson. It was a statement, not a question.

"Not if you point out that your lawyer possesses the missing information that you recorded, and you instructed them to release it to the media if anything happens to you," Archer noted. "If she asks, just refuse to explain what it is because that's your ace in the hole."

Anderson thought about it for a while, then sighed and nodded in resignation. "A deadman's switch? OK. That might work. When it's done, then I'm gone." At least Anderson was perceptive enough to do the math in his head and quickly figure out it was a decent enough plan to work.

Archer nodded, a half-smile forming on his face. "Agreed."

Neither me nor Archer saw fit to tell Anderson we had both filmed and recorded everything Anderson had just said to us. It was our own version of a deadman's switch.

* * *

"Why us?" Riley asked, confused.

"Because nobody we're investigating has any idea what either of you look like. Or that you even exist," Archer replied.

I snorted. "You did say you wanted to play a bigger role in the investigations. Being an unknown operative to keep an eye on things at the meeting site would be pretty helpful."

Riley and Jeffrey exchanged concerned looks. "And Yaya will be watching Mary while we're barhopping?" Jeffrey asked.

Archer nodded. "Yep. We're getting the whole family involved on this surveillance outing. Joel and Natalie will be doing some sketchy stuff for the investigation while the rest of us keep an eye on the meet and greet with the suspect."

Riley looked confused. "Sketchy stuff? He's always doing sketchy stuff. And won't your suspect recognize both of you? She's seen you before."

I smiled. "We're changing our appearance before we go to the pub."

Riley and Jeffrey burst out laughing. "Like Halloween? You two can go as a ghost and goblin," Riley managed to chuckle.

Archer snorted a small laugh. "Something like that."

CHAPTER 9

"I'm in," Joel said over his mic. He was working quickly and put the wire cutter back into his tool bag.

Joel's earpiece registered a click that served as Natalie's acknowledgment. She was walking their dog past the outside of the residence as a ruse since she was the lookout.

He pushed the back gate open. Minutes earlier, Joel had thoroughly sprayed the hinges with silicon to ensure they worked soundlessly after he bypassed the security system. Thanks to Archer's keen observation when we visited Samantha Triton's residence, Archer had identified the manufacturer of the system. That information enabled Joel to research how to bypass the system without triggering any faults. To the company monitoring the alarms, nothing appeared to be amiss and Joel wouldn't appear on any video. For tonight's purposes, he was just a phantom.

To that end, Joel quickly approached the main residence. He could see lights and shadows inside as the staff went about their duties, so Joel slunk around to the darkest side of the home and kept out of sight.

"Bingo," Joel muttered to himself. As he had hoped, there was a side door hidden in the darkness on the east side of the residence. Joel tried the door handle, and was mildly surprised to find the door was unlocked. Slipping inside, he found himself in a well-lit, ample-sized mudroom.

Scanning his surroundings, Joel scratched at his thick, dark beard while he recalled Archer's detailed description of the home's main floor layout. Joel moved to the open doorway leading into the interior and listened. The staff sounded far from the mudroom, so Joel risked a quick peek into the hall beyond. It was empty.

He quietly walked into the hall and turned right, towards the back of the home, which faced the lakefront. He moved quickly and found the glass doors opening into the home office. It was a large, well-appointed office with a mahogany desk and tastefully decorated bookshelves lining two of the walls. The third was a window wall through which Joel could see the moon reflecting off the rippling waves of Lake Minnetonka.

Closing the doors behind him, Joel moved to stand behind the expansive desk. He pulled a small surveillance bug out of his pocket and taped it to the underside of the desk. Just then, he could hear the clickety-clacking of hard-soled shoes walking towards the office on the tile surface of the outer hall. Joel ducked down and crawled inside the space normally occupied by the chair, and he pulled the chair back in as far as he could. Seconds later, the doors to the office opened and the footsteps approached the desk. Whoever it was dropped some things, perhaps a package and a bundle of mail, onto the desk, and walked out of the office.

His heart beating rapidly, Joel quietly pushed the chair away and crawled out of the desk. Making himself small enough to fit the confined space was an impressive feat for a 6-foot, 4-inch man, but he wouldn't have been able to maintain the position for long.

Quietly leaving the office, Joel again followed the directions Archer had given him and soon found himself passing through the large, indoor garden in the back of the property. Twice he had to hide in the foliage to avoid being seen by the servants. Not being a botanist, Joel paid little attention to the plants other than to note that several seemed vaguely exotic and one left an oily residue on his arm that didn't seem to brush off easily.

By the time the gardener and other staff had passed by on their return trips into the rest of the home, Joel had decided to stay off the path as long as possible. He carefully and methodically found a route, taking time to move plants as little as possible to avoid alerting anyone that someone was lurking in the foliage. Eventually, Joel arrived at the glass-walled sitting room positioned atop the garden structure. His arm was starting to burn and itch where the oily residue was still coating his skin. Ignoring that, Joel slipped into the so-called "sunroom" and looked around. The room was surprisingly well lit by the moon and the lights of homes along the shore of Lake Minnetonka that were twinkling across the ripples in the water. The dramatic views of the garden and lake held his attention for a few moments before he got to work. There was plenty of comfortable furniture in the room for him to place the next bug where it wouldn't be spotted.

"Subject is 60 seconds out," Natalie suddenly said through the earpiece in Joel's left ear. She had maintained radio silence during Joel's incursion while she walked their dog along the only road leading into the neighborhood, but now she alerted him that he was out of time. After making sure the garden was empty again, Joel silently exited the sunroom. Joel heard the sound of the gardener returning as he slipped through a door leading from the garden into the darkness of the back yard. Scratching his arm, he had to move quickly. He had only 30 seconds to disappear or risk getting exposed.

Headlights turned into the driveway. They belonged to the type of British supercar that a mechanically inclined car fanboy like Joel would daydream about driving, but he didn't have time to admire Samantha Triton's ride. Joel vanished into the shrubbery near the back gate by the shoreline, his grubby old camouflage clothing melding perfectly into the bushes. Then he lay still while watching the car pull into the garage because its headlights threw plenty of light in his direction for a few moments.

As soon as the lights flicked off and darkness returned, Joel darted out the back gate and made his way to the deserted public access that was a quarter mile down the shoreline. Natalie and their dog were waiting for him there. Handing Joel a backpack, Natalie kept lookout while Joel quickly changed into more stylish clothing to fit better in their current surroundings. Joel quickly stuffed his grubby clothes into the bottom of the backpack and packed various bags of dog food, new waste bags, and water bottles over the top. He also washed off his arm in the cool water of the lake. Joel scrubbed forearm with sand and water until the burning and itching subsided, which took longer than they would have liked. They really wanted to be elsewhere.

Joel and Natalie quietly held hands and strolled for about a mile to another section of the residential development. They looked like any other wealthy young couple walking their dog long after dinner but before bedtime, and seemed in no particular hurry to get anywhere.

That facade ended as soon as a small Toyota nearly screeched to a stop next to them. With the window rolled down, Riley half hissed and half snapped, "Get in!" As soon as they piled in, the car pulled away.

Joel laughed. "Really? You're using your annoyed "Get up! We're late for school," tone?" he said.

Riley snorted, but didn't take her eyes off the road. "I missed being able to yell at you to get up for school because you were making us late. Every. Single. Morning."

Natalie burst out laughing. "He's still not a morning person!"

Changing subjects, Riley said, "I had to race over here from Dad and Archer's stakeout of Samantha at Forty-Three Gallons. So it kind of reminds me of when Joel made us late for school."

The sound of a phone ringing coincided with the appearance of an incoming call on Riley's car screen. "Yes?" she answered. She saw it was an unregistered number, but picked up because she was expecting a call from a burner phone.

"Riley, this is Archer. Was the package delivered?"

Joel answered for the group. "Yes. It was gift wrapped and delivered," he said cryptically. "We're in the wind."

Earlier, Archer and Joel had agreed upon "gift wrapped and delivered," as their code for successfully planting the surveillance bug in Samantha Triton's home office and glass walled sunroom.

"Good. I'll get to work. See you guys back at the ranch," Archer said. The call ended.

"What do you think they'll find?" Riley asked absently as she accelerated up the ramp and merged with traffic on Highway 169. "Investment tips or something? She's a gazillionaire."

Joel shrugged. "Dad and Archer were keeping tight lipped about why this was so important. I asked Annabelle, and all she said was Samantha Triton isn't who she seems to be. That's it."

"Maybe they'll spill the beans at family dinner next weekend?" Natalie said.

Natalie didn't know then how prophetic her theory was.

* * *

Without needing to look, I could feel big, sad, eyes staring morosely, aching with an acute hunger. Moments later, something cold and wet brushed against my knee. Looking down, I watched Bandito as he tried to nonchalantly flop his big, furry head right into my lap.

Seeing this play out, Joel barked a laugh. "Don't fall for that. It's a trap!" He chuckled as he scratched the gauze bandage wrapped around his forearm for a moment.

Looking annoyed, Natalie brushed Joel's hand away. "Stop scratching! It needs to heal."

The entire family was gathered around our dining table eating spaghetti made with my wife Heidi's homemade meat sauce that everyone always raves about. Joel and Natalie brought their medium-large, light brown mutt named Waffles over. Their oddball dog had earned her name because she would go counter surfing specifically to steal waffles, but never anything else. Annabelle and Emily had brought 85 pounds of furry Bandito along. The big klutz had yet to grow mature enough to realize he was a high energy, house hippo who scrambled around when he was excited and bowled people over like a cartoon dog. They joined Puff Ball, Riley and Jeffrey's Husky, so we had reached peak fur in the house this evening.

Riley laughed. "You're the weak link, Dad. Bandito knows that." She took a bite of spaghetti before breaking up a piece of garlic bread to place on Mary's plate.

Snorting in barely suppressed laughter, Archer took a sip of his beer before grabbing another piece of garlic bread as the basket was being passed around the table. "Every dog we pass seems to run right up to Dante like they're best friends. Weirdest damn thing I've ever seen." Months ago, Archer began joining in our family dinners and he was sitting in his usual seat at the table.

Making air quotes, Riley quipped, "Dad once quipped he's 'One With The Canines.' Turns out he wasn't kidding," she remarked.

"Hey, I'm right here, you know," I said. It felt a little like they had forgotten I was still in the room while talking trash about me. I looked down and suddenly realized at my feet were three sets of sad canine eyes staring expectantly back at me. Puff Ball's tongue licked her chops for dramatic effect. I slipped chunks of garlic bread to all three dogs and shooed them away.

"So, did our little adventure turn anything up?" asked Joel, drawing out the first word of his sentence. Since he was the one who took the biggest risk in the operation, he was naturally curious as to whether those risks were worth it.

Pursing his lips and raising his eyebrows, Archer nodded. "Jackpot. Sure helps to have, uh, talents like yours around. Comes in handy."

Heidi's voice floated in from the kitchen. "I don't wanna hear that. He needs to use his powers for good!"

Everyone laughed. Heidi telling our kids to use their powers for good has been something she's joked about since Joel was a little lawn monster who frequently would sneak out of bed to ask Heidi if she wanted to snuggle on the couch and watch football with him.

"We'll play some of the juicier parts we recorded after the kids are off to bed," Annabelle said. "But suffice it to say, now we have a lead."

The next hour and a half passed quickly, and several bottles of red wine were sacrificed by the time everyone settled down around the dinner table again. While I refilled Annabelle's glass, Jerry Tavington had arrived. Annabelle set a portable speaker on the table and synced her laptop to it. Soon, she was ready.

"Alright, the short version is we solved a murder," Annabelle announced theatrically. "Problem is, it's just not the murder we were hired to solve. On the bright side, we now have some leads we hope will help us solve what we were hired to solve. Take a listen. It's one side of a phone call."

> *Tammy, it's Sam. We have a problem with Ryan.*
>
> *…*
>
> *No. Worse than just a problem. He's going to link us to both Erik Johnson's death and Bill Harrison's. Someone's got something on him and the bastard thinks he can save his skin by giving us up.*
>
> *…*
>
> *No. I don't think sleeping with Ryan again and letting him get one of us pregnant is going to change his mind.*
>
> *…*
>
> *You can pass off a pregnancy because your husband is still around. Martin doesn't get conjugal visits. I get pregnant and I lose control of the company.*
>
> *…*
>
> *It's in the prenup between me and Martin.*
>
> *…*

*Ryan claims he has some sort of fail-safe to release docu-
ments if he turns up dead or missing. I think he called it a
deadman's switch. I don't believe him.*

…

*No, they ruled his death was an accident, remember? There
was no toxicology testing in Johnson's autopsy. You know
that.*

…

*I think we gotta eliminate Ryan. Like with Johnson and
Harrison.*

Annabelle stopped the playback and looked at all the surprised faces
with raised eyebrows around the dinner table. "Well?" She asked.

Tavington was the first to speak. "Was that who I think it was?"

Archer nodded. "Yep. Samantha Triton. Speaking to her and Ryan
Anderson's shared lover, Tammy Kettle. She …" he was saying when Tavington interrupted.

"How the hell did you get that recording?" Tavington demanded. It
was fairly likely he might be called upon to defend the podcast in court
if we played it on air. Tavington would need to have figured out what to
say and how we should present it before that happened.

I took this one. "While we were staking out and recording Anderson's confrontation with Triton at Forty-Three Gallons of Whiskey
Brewing Company up in Minnetonka, an enterprising person planted
surveillance bugs in Samantha's home office and garden sunroom." I said
it matter-of-factly, without any emotion whatsoever.

Tavington's eyes fluttered and rolled back slightly while he took a
deep breath to calm himself. "You're going to get …" he was saying when
Archer interrupted him.

"With permission of the homeowner, naturally," Archer stated. He
was intently looking at Tavington to gauge his reaction.

Tavington's reaction was one of sudden confusion for a few moments while he did the math in his head. Suddenly he asked, "Martin?"

Smiling coldly, I said, "Yes. Martin expressly gave us permission to bug his own house. In writing."

A smile slowly spread over Tavington's face. "No shit? So, it wasn't an actual case of trespassing?"

I shook my head. "Nope. We checked the title on the property. It's in his name only. And the prenup specifies that the property stays his and his alone. And there's more. If Samantha strays or they divorce, the prenup specifies the company shares will pass to Terry Triton, not Samantha. She'll be out."

"Geez, Dante. Looks like we've solved the mystery," Tavington remarked.

Annabelle shook her head. "Only one mystery. We still have to prove who killed Harrison because that's what we were actually hired to do."

I added, "We also sort of solved something else that confused us. Remember when Anderson told us Samantha said she wanted to send some decorative plants as a gift for Socrates? Turns out the ancient philosopher Socrates was thought to have been poisoned by hemlock, and there's no antidote for it."

Joel's eyes widened in fear at that announcement. "So, the rash on my arm from the garden wasn't poison oak?"

Archer shook his head. "No, it's poison oak and your doctor said so. You'd most likely have to eat or drink the hemlock to die from it."

Frowning, Annabelle had a thought she couldn't shake. "Wouldn't hemlock poisoning show up in a toxicology report?"

"Probably. I didn't run that down though. No toxicology report was made for Johnson because he was thought to have died by blunt force trauma to the skull. There also wasn't a toxicology report for Harrison, either," I said, thinking about what we'd heard about Martin's conviction for murdering Harrison by snapping his neck while choking him. "His death could have possibly been caused by hemlock poisoning. If toxicology reports can be run on their remains, a match could tie their deaths together."

Tavington nodded thoughtfully. "Yeah. You said for Annabelle's defense in Zoe's death, that's just the '*What*'. A 'get-outta-jail-free-card' for Martin would take a convincing explanation of exactly '*Why*' Martin wanted Harrison and Johnson alive instead of dead."

That explanation of our predicament was the crux of Martin's case. Since we secretly recorded everything, we have explanations of why Martin would want Johnson alive. By extension, Harrison would have to be alive for Johnson's role as a sort of double agent to achieve Martin's desired impact to lead Harrison down the wrong road. Martin's scheme was for Johnson to feed fables and lies to Harrison.

We knew Martin and Bill Harrison were longtime business rivals, and that it wasn't a friendly rivalry because of the industrial espionage. Both wanted to snap up their rival's business at a deep discount. Martin's best route to do so was to use Johnson as a double agent to lead Bill to make bad business decisions over a lengthy period of time, with the result of strengthening Martin's company at the expense of Harrison's. In that sense, it was easy to see '*why*' Martin needed Johnson alive.

"To figure out 'why' something happens, we need to identify who benefits from the outcome of that occurrence," I said. "Clearly Harrison did not benefit from becoming a corpse, and his death actually does not benefit Martin, either."

"Terry Triton benefits," Annabelle stated. "With our help, he finally will get control of the company."

Tavington shook his head. "Too many steps and too complicated. Terry was heir apparent and would have eventually gotten control of the company by succession when Martin stepped down for retirement. All Terry had to do was wait him out a couple of years. Because of the terms of Martin's prenuptial agreement with Samantha, Terry would have been better served by hiring us to look into her infidelity. What's more, Terry knows it as well as we do. In my book, that reduces the likelihood that Terry ended Harrison."

Archer's eyebrows arched high as he looked at Tavington. "So, either it's someone as-of-yet unknown, or its Samantha because she has something to gain."

I answered for Jerry. "Yeah, but she has the same issue that Terry would have. Too many steps and too complicated, making her ability to gain control of the company uncertain at best."

"And, we still don't know how she would have ended Harrison, or pinned his death on Martin. Harrison's death still leaves her exposed to lose it all due to the prenup's clause stripping her of ownership for infidelity," Annabelle concluded. "Unless all her plans haven't come to fruition?"

"Which means she needs to bump off Terry to close the circle. We need to warn him!" Archer exclaimed as he traded alarmed looks with Tavington.

While Tavington and Archer discussed more aspects of the investigation with Annabelle, I called Terry and told him to stay in a safe space and not to eat or drink anything that wasn't sealed by the manufacturer. Terry immediately agreed, and said he would await our arrival at his home.

* * *

"I know," Terry before he sipped from a can of sparkling water he had just opened.

Tavington's head suddenly raised to look at Terry with a look of surprise. "You *KNEW*? What do you mean you knew?"

It was the exact same question that popped into my head, so I looked hard at Terry while we waited for an answer. Other inchoate questions also swirled around, waiting to form up in some semblance of order to be articulated.

Terry's head tilted briefly to the side while he thought about how to answer. When he was ready, he spoke again. "At least, I had deduced some of what you've uncovered. Definitely not as much as you've found, but a little bit of it. Mostly suspected, I guess."

Terry's rambling answer left much to be desired, so Tavington pressed on.

"Which parts?" Tavington prompted.

"Her cheating and the prenup clause, which would throw her out of the company leadership. But that still left me with the problem you've already identified, which is that my dad would still be stuck in jail for a murder I don't think he committed."

Annabelle looked confused for a few moments. "So why didn't you tell us that when you asked for our help?"

Terry's eyebrows arched briefly. He seemed to be steeling himself for an answer he knew we wouldn't appreciate much. Then he sighed softly just before speaking. "Because I wanted you to take an unbiased look at this whole situation without being overly influenced by information from me. Had I filled you with my suspicions about this person or that person, you might've ended up shining a light in the wrong direction. And I was right to avoid influencing your investigation, because you dug up quite a bit that we did not know."

"Like what?" I asked. I didn't tell Terry that I privately agreed with his decision not to try to influence our investigation. He was right and we don't like having our time wasted.

"Ryan Anderson and Tammy Kettle's involvement. I suspected Samantha had a relationship with someone, but did not know it was with them. Or the other things those three seem to have done. Or that Johnson's death likely wasn't an accident. In fact, we hadn't given Johnson's death any thought at all because we had no idea about his connection to Harrison and about my dad's plans to use him in his version of counter-espionage," Terry said, his eyes not really focused on any place in the room at the moment while he organized his thoughts.

"Martin never told you about Johnson?" Tavington sounded incredulous.

Terry snorted. "Oh, definitely not. If something sketchy was being done in the industrial espionage world, he wouldn't breathe a word about it for fear of bringing down the wrath of the Securities and Exchange

Commission or some other alphabet agency run by the feds. As far as he is concerned, the fewer in the know, the better."

At this point, I couldn't be sure that Terry was being entirely truthful with us; however, I also didn't get the feeling that he was withholding anything from us any longer. In fact, he looked like he was still trying to process the information we had given him. That wasn't surprising since the results of our investigation contained bombshell revelations.

"What precautions are you taking for your safety?" Annabelle asked.

Terry chuffed slightly as he half-smiled and focused his eyes on Annabelle. "Mostly just an armed security guard, but nothing in the way of preventing poisoning." Frowning in concentration for a moment, he continued. "Pretty sure nobody thought of poison as something to watch out for since the coroner took one look at the corpse and ruled Harrison was killed by a dramatically broken neck."

Nodding, Tavington agreed. "Yeah. We'll need to get a court order to dig up Harrison's bones to get some toxicology tests run. If those tests show the man was ended by poisoning instead of a broken neck, then the broken neck was a red herring to hide the real cause of death. We'll need to beef up Terry's protection, though."

Terry unconsciously tilted his head slightly to the side while he thought, then he shook his head dejectedly. "Samantha won't stop gunning for me until I'm dead. All she's gotta do is find a gap in the security."

I was thunderstruck. Not by what Terry said, but by the idea his words evoked. "Maybe you can be the spider in the parlor," I said.

Everyone stopped and stared at me. Tavington was the first to speak. "That's a helluva risk to take…" His voice trailed off as he thought about it.

"Not if Samantha thinks she has to kill Terry immediately and a juicy opportunity to do that arises," Annabelle concluded. She saw where I had been headed with this line of thought.

"Then the urgency will make her be less careful," Archer said with finality. "I got an idea."

CHAPTER 10

The soft illumination of a floor lamp grudgingly lit a small circle around a favorite chair, casting long, dim shadows that disappeared into the gloom of the great room. Terry's cabin was at the far east end of a branch of a small lake that was entirely owned by the Triton family up in the north woods. All the surrounding land was likewise owned by the Triton family, who ensured their privacy by preventing construction of new roads or trails. There was just a miles-long paved road winding through the dense, mix if pines and deciduous forest from a lonely two-lane highway to the cabin, and that was it for access to the lake.

Terry Triton occupied the plush leather chair. It was his favorite spot in the secluded lake cabin, which was his longtime retreat from the struggles of the world. The four-bedroom, three-bath cabin wasn't big by Triton family standards. When Terry had it built, it was designed for easy maintenance and reflected a tasteful beauty that was both airy and quietly elegant.

He was especially proud of the kitchen. Marble subway tiles reached up to a 10-foot-high ceiling and a massive 15-foot-long island was capped by a vast expanse of polished quartzite. The kitchen featured high-end, stainless-steel appliances, a gas range with eight burners arranged around a griddle and multiple dishwashers hidden away in the pantry. The space between the kitchen and living area had been designed with entertaining in mind. It featured a tasteful, floor-to-ceiling glass door, and a refrigerated wine cellar that displayed dozens of vintages situated for easy access. Next to the "cellar" and opposite the glass wall that looked out to the lake and woods, was a wet bar with a built-in beverage fridge.

It was quiet in the cabin. For hours, the only sound was the tinkle of ice against the successive glasses of the bourbon that Terry kept sipping while he read a new book on a tablet. Terry had become so immersed in his book that he nearly leapt out of his chair when a voice suddenly intruded upon his quiet solitude. The softly spoken words seemed as blaring as a car horn.

"I brought a beverage that you should enjoy," said a woman's voice. Out of the darkness emerged a brunette, brown-eyed woman in her early 50s, holding a small drink container in her left hand and a small caliber pistol in her right. Finger on the trigger, Samantha never pointed the weapon at anything other than directly at Terry.

Terry stared at Samantha Triton for a moment before setting his bourbon down on the side table next to the easy chair. His eyes locked onto Samantha's eyes, and a disarming smile slowly appeared on his face. "Thought you might show up. What's in the bottle?"

Uncertainty caused Samantha's eyes to squint slightly. "Hemlock tea. It's for you," she said confidently. "I've always hated you, and I'm finally going to get rid of you once and for all.

"Or what? You'll shoot?" Terry said, his voice sounding dangerous now. "Was that the choice you gave Bill Harrison, too?" His eyes remained locked onto Samantha's.

Samantha sneered. "Didn't have to point a gun at him. Bill thought he was sharing a cup of ordinary tea with his stooge, Erik, while they sat in his study and plotted to take the company from me. Those fools had no idea they were about to become corpses." Her demeanor became visibly angry while she said this. "Why am I bothering to tell you? I can see the question in your eyes," she asked rhetorically.

Nodding with a slight arching of his eyebrows, Terry said, "The question did cross my mind, yes. I suppose it's because you feel a little confession is good for the soul?"

"Perhaps. Won't matter once you're gone. Make your choice, I can deal with you either way," Samantha said, clearly making an effort to sound nonchalant.

Terry flashed a broad smile that was completely incongruous to the situation he found himself in. "Nah, I'm fine as is. We don't think you're in any position to call the shots now."

Samantha's head tilted slightly to the right in a mixture of annoyance and confusion. "We? Who's 'we'?"

"Me. And them," he said quietly while pointing past Samantha with his chin.

From the dark gloom beyond the small light came the unmistakable sound of a shotgun shell being chambered. Samantha froze and looked over her shoulder at two shadows that she belatedly realized were slightly darker than the surrounding gloom.

Annabelle and Archer emerged into the light. The gas-operated, semi-automatic 12 gauge in Archer's hands was planted into his right shoulder and pointed straight at Samantha. His finger resting on the trigger, Archer stepped to his right during his approach to ensure a clear line of fire at Samantha so he wouldn't hit Terry. Annabelle likewise had her finger on the trigger of the small 9mm pistol and had her weapon aimed at Samantha as well. Annabelle had owned the gun for years and practiced shooting with it extensively.

"Be a good girl and set those on the floor behind you. Slowly, mind you. Mr. Archer hasn't shot anyone lately so he's a bit trigger happy," Annabelle said.

The look of complete shock on Samantha's face was priceless.

* * *

"Why?" Ryan Anderson asked, a look of confusion painted on his face as he stared in confusion at the blonde, blue-eyed woman in her mid-50s who pointed a small caliber pistol at him.

"Why? Because you're going to sell us out, that's why!" hissed Tammy Kettle. She was breathing heavily, and the adrenaline coursing through her veins caused her hands to shake slightly.

They were standing in Anderson's house in Minnetonka. It was an older Craftsman home that had been extensively updated prior to Anderson's acquisition of it. While the vintage high-end fixtures and countertops were among the renovations that originally drew him to buy the home, he had come to appreciate the unseen improvements that had been made when the original walls and plaster had been renovated. Modern electrical and plumbing made the residence safer, and the addition of spray foam insulation and new windows kept the temperature comfortable despite the extremes of Minnesota weather. On the surface, the extensive work was beautiful and period appropriate for the structure. Great care had been taken to reuse and refurbish original materials when possible. The result looked old and well cared for despite the reality that much of the home was essentially new.

Anderson looked down at the pistol held by Kettle, his right eyebrow arching slightly. "So you think you're just going to shoot me with that thing? And then what? Just fuck off back into the world like nothing happened?"

Kettle's blue eyes narrowed slightly. "How'd you guess?" she said sarcastically. The pistol in her hand was still shaking slightly.

"Can't even do me the courtesy of poison? Kill me the same way you did Erik Johnson and Bill Harrison?" Anderson said slowly. His eyes remained locked onto Kettle's.

Kettle snorted derisively. "I didn't kill Erik. That was all Samantha."

Tilting his head to the left slightly, Anderson asked, "Then why are you here? Breaking into a man's home and pointing a gun at him isn't the behavior of someone with nothing to hide."

Kettle's expression changed to one of disbelief for a moment before anger overrode everything else. "What? How about fuck you!" she snarled. Then she pulled the trigger.

Inside the house, the shot was deafening. Anderson was knocked down onto his knees as he tumbled over in agony.

Kettle lowered her arm holding the pistol, almost as if she were surprised at the result of pulling the trigger. Then the expression on her face turned to alarm as she looked for blood and didn't find any. Her ears rang so loudly, she didn't hear the sounds of boots running on the floor behind her, so she was completely unprepared to be tackled from behind by a large man. Moments after Kettle's head was slammed into the floor, she groaned in a complex mix of fear, pain and surprise as her hands were roughly handcuffed behind her.

Once the police detective motioned for the arresting officer to pull her into a sitting position on the floor with her legs splayed in front of her, she looked up at the men surrounding her. Her face expressed absolute shock as she recognized me standing next to the Minnetonka police detective. I removed the ear plugs I had been wearing in case she fired a gun in the house.

"You!" she screeched, and she rolled onto her knees in a sudden attempt to rise to her feet despite her hands being cuffed behind her. She lost her balance and tottered over, crashing back to the hardwood floor. No one moved to help her.

Shooting mc a sardonic look when Kettle lost her balance, Detective David Deroshier snorted and shook his head slightly. "Another satisfied customer of yours, Dante?" he quipped. It was a statement, not a question, that was made more satirical by flashing strobe lights of emergency vehicles pulling up in front of the home.

"Pretty sure she's *your* customer now, Dave. We—" I had begun saying when a groan rising from the floor interrupted me. We both turned to look at Anderson, who was being helped to a sitting position by another officer.

"Good morning, Sleeping Beauty. Did you get a nice nap in while we arrested the bad guys?" Deroshier asked, keeping his sarcastic tone.

Anderson shot Deroshier a pained look of annoyance as he slowly reached up to begin unzipping his sweatshirt. "Oh man, that shit hurts!" he moaned while he removed the sweatshirt to reveal the body armor he wore underneath.

Deroshier snorted a laugh as he squatted down next to Anderson and used a gloved hand to quickly pluck the flattened bullet from Anderson's vest.

"Hey! I wanted to keep …" Anderson was protesting weakly when Deroshier interrupted him.

"It's evidence. You can get it back after Mrs. Kettle's trial," Deroshier said with a tilt of his head towards where she was lying face down on the floor. She was breathing hard with an angry expression on her face. She turned her head slightly to glare at Deroshier through her tangled blonde hair.

Anderson looked at me for a moment before his eyes focused on the ear plugs I was holding. "You brought ear plugs?" he said. "You said there shouldn't be any shooting!"

I half-smiled, ruefully. "Shouldn't doesn't mean won't." Just then, my cell phone rang. I broke eye contact with Anderson and fished the phone out of my pocket and answered. "Hey kiddo, any luck?" I asked.

"Dad, we got Samantha. Archer cuffed her to a tree where he can keep an eye on her until the sheriff arrives. I just watched the video of Anderson and Kettle. It's gonna be lit when we play it on the next episode!" Annabelle exclaimed breathlessly. The hidden high definition cameras we had installed recorded the attempted murder and she had streamed the video to her phone.

"Oh yeah. That's perfect! Let's get the team together tomorrow and we'll work on the show," I said before Annabelle hung up. I could just imagine what a kerfuffle the next episode of the show would cause.

CHAPTER 11

"Murder in Minnesota," The Trifecta of Terror episode excerpt:

[Archer] That's right, Annabelle. What we found was a really confusing situation. Terry Triton hired us to investigate the conviction of his father, Martin, the CEO of Triton Industries in Minnetonka, for the murder of billionaire Bill Harrison. Martin had been convicted of murdering his business rival, Bill Harrison by breaking his neck. Reviewing the trial evidence and transcripts really was astonishing, because the State's theory about how Martin supposedly broke Harrison's neck just did not make sense to us.

[Annabelle] Mr. Archer, can you explain how it never made sense?

[Archer] The State argued Martin, a senior citizen, simply snapped Harrison's neck using his bare hands. Killing a person that way is basically an overused TV and movie trope that is inexplicably portrayed as one of the surest ways to kill someone. Problem is, it isn't very plausible, especially for an old guy like Martin.

[Annabelle] Mr. Finch, why didn't Martin's attorneys point that out at trial? Surely they would have at least addressed that issue somewhat?"

[Dante] Honestly, I have no idea. The transcripts seemed to suggest Martin's high-priced defense counsel were completely surprised by the State's broken neck theory. Even more oddly, they didn't seem nimble enough to simply introduce the obvious that was staring them right in the face. Martin is 68 years old and walks with a cane. Making the theory even more inexplicable is the fact that Martin has significant pain and weakness in his left hand from a bone chip injury to the left wrist when he was a teenager playing for the school basketball team. That ...

[Annabelle] Wouldn't that make it harder to snap Harrison's neck when choking him, then?"

[Dante] Oh yes, clearly. Nor did the State or defense counsel address the absence of any signs of left side weakness in the choking of Harrison that led to his broken neck. There was just nothing at all. It's as if prosecutors simply pointed at the senior citizen with a walking cane seated at the defense table and then demanded the jury convict the guy by pretending he somehow possessed the superhuman strength needed to accidentally snap a younger man's neck while trying to choke him out. So there definitely were irregularities in establishing the means of Harrison's death. The motive was also sussed out improperly.

[Annabelle] Improperly? How so?

[Dante] While the simplest theory is usually the best for trial strategy because it presents the easiest story to tell, this time the truth turned out to be more complicated than that.

[Archer] Sure did. The story told by the State was that Harrison's death was a simple case of murdering a business rival. The truth we uncovered is much murkier. Thanks to recently completed toxicology testing, we now know Harrison actually died from hemlock poisoning. But, in an effort to cover up poisoning as the true cause of his death and lead the medical examiner to conclude toxicology testing was unnecessary, Harrison's neck had been broken after he died.

[Annabelle] Poisoning! So does that mean Martin Triton is innocent?

[Dante] No, not by itself. It's certainly an appealable issue, but all it means is that the State failed to prove the actual cause of death. The State would have to retry Martin and establish that he purportedly poisoned Harrison. But, the mysteries don't stop there.

[Annabelle] Mr. Finch, what else doesn't add up?

[Dante] There's another corpse at play here. Corpse number two is Erik Johnson. He visited Harrison's home the night of Harrison's death. Johnson's remains weren't discovered until several months after Harrison's demise, and then it was only because they were found floating in Lake Minnetonka.

[Archer] Johnson worked in the financial department at Triton Industries. However, Martin and his security chief, Ryan Anderson, discovered Johnson was actually an industrial espionage agent employed by Harrison. Martin then turned Johnson into a double agent and sought to use him to feed Harrison false information in an attempt to bring down Harrison's company. To accomplish that goal, it was

clearly in Martin's best interests to keep both Johnson and Harrison alive.

[Annabelle] How would Martin keep Johnson on his team then?

[Dante] A two-pronged approach was used to control Johnson. Firstly, Martin gave Johnson a financial stake in Triton Industries that would become significantly more valuable if they were successful against Harrison's company. Secondly, to seal the deal, Martin's wife, Samantha Triton, helped maintain control of Johnson through sex.

[Annabelle] But that plan went south, didn't it? What happened?

[Archer] It gets murkier here, but the bottom line is we think it has to do with controlling Martin's company shares and preventing discovery of the scheme by tying up loose ends. The prenuptial agreement between Martin and Mrs. Triton specifies that Martin's property stays his and his alone. And there's more. In the event of Mrs. Triton's infidelity or divorce, the prenup specifies the company shares will pass to Terry Triton, not Mrs. Triton. She would be out of both power and money.

Well, in this episode, we will play portions of secret recordings between Ryan Anderson, Samantha Triton and Tammy Kettle. The audio recordings clearly establish the three of them were involved in a love triangle, that Samantha and Tammy had some sort of involvement in the deaths of Harrison and Johnson, and that the two women plotted to kill Anderson to keep him from talking.

[Annabelle] Why would Samantha and Tammy want Harrison and Johnson dead? I don't understand Tammy Kettle's involvement.

[Dante] Thanks to SEC records we obtained a few weeks ago, Tammy Kettle made a huge purchase of heavily discounted Triton Industries stock prior to that company's acquisition of Harrison's company. Despite their murders, both Johnson and Harrison had still lived just long enough for Martin's plan to bring down the stock price of Harrison's company. That success meant it had become feasible for Triton Industries to go forward with a hostile takeover after several months of steady decline in the stock price of Harrison's company.

[Annabelle] Discounted? Like Triton Industries ran a 20 percent off sale or something?

[Archer] Samantha used her influence with Martin to enable the sale of shares at a discounted price. Sometimes large companies do something similar to knock off a few percent to sweeten the deal for employee stock purchase plans, but this was well beyond that. Samantha enabled the sale of 100,000 shares at a 50 percent discount to $250 per share. After the takeover of Harrison's company, the current price of those Triton shares is $1,500 per share, so Tammy made a hefty profit just on principal. Factor in the quarterly dividend, and Tammy had quite a financial interest in helping Samantha keep the secrets.

[Annabelle] If it wasn't in Martin's interest to end Harrison and Johnson, why did Martin get convicted of their murder? That seems like a loose end.

[Dante] Well, the loose end was actually Martin himself. He discovered Samantha's other infidelities after the take-over and prior stock sale to Kettle, and both Harrison and Johnson were dead. Martin confronted Samantha about it, and even learned to his horror that Samantha was the wizard behind the curtain for all of it.

[Annabelle] Infidelities? As in plural?

[Dante] Turns out not only was Samantha in a ménage à trois with Ryan Anderson and Tammy Kettle, and she was being used to sexually control Johnson, but she also was a spurned lover of Harrison's. We have recorded testimony of multiple witnesses to their liaisons. Eventually, Samantha and Harrison had a falling out, all of which took place during Samantha and Martin's marriage. She discovered Martin was going to use the infidelity clause of their pre-nuptial agreement to cut her out of both money and power, so Samantha and Tammy had to act.

The plan they hatched framed Martin for Harrison's murder. Since they had access to Harrison's DNA, it wasn't difficult to plant evidence of Harrison's blood on Martin's clothing and in his vehicle. A quick anonymous tip to law enforcement, and Martin was under arrest. Despite being taken into custody, Martin chose to keep the financial shenanigans quiet in an effort to evade SEC scrutiny in a calculated risk that he could beat the rap at the murder trial, but he chose poorly.

[Annabelle] How did Tammy and Samantha get Johnson and Harrison to ingest the poison?

[Dante] Samantha used her knowledge of the staff working in the Harrison household to direct delivery of the hem-

lock-laced tea. It was a horribly imprecise weapon of choice because there was no way to aim it beyond knowing that Harrison enjoyed tea each evening. Unfortunately, Johnson had chosen that evening to visit Harrison, and they both drank the tea.

This created a bit of a problem for Samantha and Kettle because they now had two men who had died the same way on their hands. They then brought in Ryan Anderson to help them dispose of the bodies. Samantha still had key codes to gain entry to Harrison's home because Harrison hadn't thought to change them after they were no longer sleeping together. The three snuck into his study and removed the bodies before Harrison's staff could discover them and they staged their deaths in separate locations.

The trio then decided to make it appear as if Harrison died from a broken neck and Johnson from blunt force trauma to skull instead of poisoning. Their scheme worked and Martin was convicted of Harrison's death despite the physical implausibility of Martin killing Harrison that way. Anderson stuck around long enough to help entrap Mrs. Kettle when she broke into his home to kill him a while back. Since then, Anderson cashed out at least $20 million of his company stock and he is now in the wind. I have a feeling he'll never be heard from again.

[Annabelle] So what happens now?

[Archer] Trials for Mrs. Kettle and Mrs. Triton, plus an upcoming appeal for Martin's release. "Murder in Minnesota" will be there to stay on top of developments.

CHAPTER 12

"Dead? How?" exclaimed Annabelle, speaking into her phone. She listened intently to the response to her question. "Suicide? Seriously? And the coroner already ruled it was suicide? Interesting how the coroner could rule it was suicide that fast — the corpse still had to be warm." Annabelle paused to listen further. "Mmmhmm. There were two cameras recording video of her cell 24 hours a day. What did they show?"

Annabelle's eye roll was so intense I feared she was risking ocular nerve injury. "They malfunctioned? That's what they said? *Both* cameras? How convenient. And they miraculously resumed normal function about an hour later? Interesting. Where were the two guards? Uh huh. No, I'll save you a call, they're right here looking at me."

Archer and I traded suspicious glances. Video cameras outside the cell of a high-profile suspect never "just" malfunction, especially when that suspect's life has been threatened and she is under surveillance by two guards.

Annabelle ended the call. "Who was that?" asked Archer.

"Detective Deroshier," Annabelle said smugly, satisfied with the looks of complete surprise that appeared on our faces. "He wanted us to know immediately, and said he was going to call you as soon as he got off the phone with me. I told him I'd break the news since you were right here."

Archer and I traded concerned glances. While Deroshier has been feeding us information for the show, he normally sends it through myself or Jerry Tavington so we can decide what to do with it from a legal perspective. Obviously Deroshier decided this bombshell news was important enough to send directly to Annabelle. He wasn't wrong about that.

"If I followed your end of the conversation correctly, Mrs. Triton supposedly committed suicide?" Archer asked.

"Allegedly. And the coroner immediately ruled it a suicide about as soon as her body arrived at the medical examiner's office," Annabelle noted cynically. "Hung herself with bed sheets."

"The afternoon she was changing her plea in exchange for all sorts of juicy dirt on various players also happens to be the day she manages to hang herself with some sheets before breakfast? What did the coroner rule was the cause of death? Linen poisoning?" I grumbled in disbelief.

Just then, my burner phone rang. It was an unknown number, which wasn't surprising.

"Hello?" I answered.

"Hello, my friend. I have some news you're gonna want to hear," said the now-familiar voice of Tony Sorvino. "You've heard about Samantha Triton, yes?"

"Yeah, we just got the news about her. To call it highly dubious would be an understatement." The cynicism in my voice emphasized my words.

"There's more. Tammy Kettle's dead. Presumably. I don't have a lot of details, just that she was alone, at home and her husband was working."

"Presumably?" I asked, confused. "How much presumption are we talking?"

"My guys tell me her leg with the ankle monitor was still at the house. The rest of her, who knows?"

Now I was really confused. "Why the hell would the leg with the ankle monitor still attached be left behind?"

Annabelle and Archer's faces appeared shocked by my question. I couldn't grab more of their undivided attention now if I tried.

"I dunno, but my guess is that someone was sending a message and keeping the cops guessing at the same time. As far as the monitoring service knew, she was still home, but actually only her leg was still there."

I snorted. "Well, that's just great. Rumor mill said she was turning State's witness in exchange for a sweet deal, but I don't have specifics around that."

"Me either. Very bad for business. The hitters behind this have some bad mojo. Anything more comes up, I'll pass it along. Goodbye, my friend." The normally gregarious Sorvino sounded anything but unconcerned, which was a sure sign he was nervous.

As soon as the call ended, Archer tilted his head towards me. "Spill it," he commanded.

"That was Tony Sorvino. He asked if we had heard about Samantha, and told me Tammy Kettle is probably dead somewhere," I summarized.

"Probably? Don't they know?" Annabelle asked.

"Sorvino said Kettle's leg with the ankle monitor attached to it was found at her home, but the rest of her is gone. That means it'll be a while until a window for her death is worked out. This delays the investigation because the trail as to her whereabouts is colder because of that." I shook my head slightly. "Also possibly puts Sorvino in a bit of a bind, but we can't be sure because we don't know if she's told the prosecutors what she knows yet. Kettle's death could make him a suspect if she's already told the prosecutors about him. If not, he's still in a bind because her death is bad for his business."

Archer grunted in a low laugh. "Damned if he doesn't, and damned if he does. Nice."

"So someone with something to hide decided to erase the prime witnesses. Well, that just sucks," Annabelle grumbled.

Looking at Annabelle, Archer nodded slightly. "Especially for the witnesses. Someone connected enough to rub out two high-profile targets has gotta be especially dangerous. The kind of hitter who can take a player off the board despite being under guard inside a jail isn't someone we'd want to tangle with."

With that, the three of us just looked at each other for a moment before Annabelle broke the silence with the inevitable question. "Who stands to gain from killing Samantha and Tammy?"

I shrugged, then retrieved the coffee pot to pour another round of bitter motivation for us while Archer and Annabelle thought about it. "I'm going to take Sorvino out of the mix for the moment. It seems too obvious that he both gains and loses from the death of Tammy, but he wouldn't have the need to also take out Samantha. Way I see it, the negative side of the ledger then outweighs the positive side for him. What's more, him calling with the news tells me he already knows Tammy's death isn't a good thing for him. Sorvino may be a mobster but he's not stupid."

"*May*be? He definitely is a mobster. But I think you're right about him. Smart and cagey. Knows who he can trust. He isn't likely to be the hitter here," Archer mused. "What about Terry?"

"Oof. That's a hard one. Taking out Samantha obviously benefits him for control of the company. Problem is, he's already achieved that benefit due to the infidelity clause in the prenuptial agreement. Her demise just creates new problems for him without bringing any new benefits that I can see," I said before taking a sip of the coffee.

Annabelle wondered aloud for a moment. "Wouldn't Martin benefit from Samantha's death?"

Archer tilted his head to the side as he shrugged. "Well, he would. But he's now regained the company shares from Samantha due to the operation of the infidelity clause in his prenuptial agreement with her, so that negates any benefit to him. He also didn't have a reason to end Tammy, as Tammy's death wouldn't be helpful to him."

"Taking it a bit further, Samantha and Tammy's deaths before the hearing on his attorney's motion to overturn the sentencing negatively impacts Martin's interests in getting out of prison. I'm thinking Martin isn't the culprit," I added. Moments later, a new thought struck me. "What about Ryan Anderson?"

Arching his eyebrows, Archer sighed slightly while his eyes drifted off to scrutinize the ceiling without really looking at it. "Anderson could have a bit to gain by taking both ladies off the board. Eliminating their unrecorded testimony might make it more difficult to convict him of certain major crimes should he be captured. But it wouldn't affect his culpability for some lesser crimes."

We kicked around a few more ideas for a while, but no one seemed more likely than the missing Ryan Anderson. The problem for us is that Anderson's potential gain didn't seem particularly important for someone with independent wealth and nothing meaningful to anchor him to Minnesota.

* * *

The courthouse is located in the Hennepin County Government Center in Minneapolis. It's the manifestation of a mid-1970s idea of what a government administration building ought to look like. The result was an unremarkable, 24-story, edifice to bureaucracy that takes on the appearance of the letter 'H' when viewed from the northeast or southwest. The ends of the building are two towers connected by a series of catwalks and enclosed by glass windows to form an atrium.

Archer, Annabelle and I were walking towards the Hennepin County Courthouse when we spotted a crowd of reporters blocking access to the building entrance. Archer and I exchanged looks with Annabelle, who rolled her eyes at us in exasperation. She had no trouble figuring were totally going to throw her under the media bus, which is what Archer and I usually did because we were good at it and it was kind of fun.

I chuffed with dark humor. "Hey, you're the face of the operation. Ain't nobody want to see old guys like us filling their screens."

"Yeah, especially a lawyer's. The horror!" Archer moaned facetiously.

"Agreed. Makes you wanna throw up in your mouth a little," I quipped, then looked around for a few moments before sighing. "Time to go to work." Trudging into a courthouse seemed like a terrible waste of a perfectly beautiful late September morning. The sky was blue, and the crisp air promised a beautiful fall filled with a riot of changing colors.

Much like tripping someone to distract a zombie horde with a convenient snack, Archer and I used Annabelle to occupy the cameras and reporters so we could slip into the courthouse unmolested. Neither of us was surprised by the media attention. The conviction of prominent billionaire Martin Triton for the murder of a rival billionaire had generated keen interest in the case long before we were ever hired to look into it. Our investigation had only helped keep that interest alive. There's nothing that grabs media attention like stories filled with salacious sex, money, power, betrayal and murder.

Soon, we were settled next to Terry Triton in the courtroom gallery where Martin's hearing would be argued. A grave-looking Terry shook our hands in greeting and whispered, "I don't even know why this hearing is going forward today. Dad's lawyers filed a motion for a continuance, but the judge denied it."

"I can't imagine why Judge Emhoff wouldn't grant the motion. Two of the prime culprits for the murder were themselves just killed, and one of them was in State custody when it happened. Something's off here," I said quietly.

Terry nodded, his face looking somehow more serious now. "I'm afraid you're right."

The appearance of the bailiff put an end to our conversation. "Everyone please rise! The District Court of the Fourth Judicial District, County of Hennepin, State of Minnesota is now open. Judge Barry Emhoff presiding," announced the bailiff loudly.

The attorneys and media in attendance stood for Judge Emhoff as he walked to the bench at the front of his courtroom, and they resumed their seats when the bailiff said they could. In his late 50s, Emhoff had gray hair and bushy salt-and-pepper eyebrows shading his dark brown eyes. He has a reputation for being crusty and grouchy on the best of days. A law school graduate of the University of Wisconsin, Emhoff has sat on the bench over 25 years after leaving a large law firm in downtown Minneapolis. He has four children and has been married to his wife, Patty, for over 35 years. For the past five years, Emhoff has acted as Chief Judge of the fourth judicial circuit court. Our sources reported that he constantly feels harried and overworked, and was now marking time to hit the requisite number of years of service to retire.

"Good morning. Attorney Calwis, it's your motion hearing seeking to reverse the conviction of Mr. Triton. Are you prepared to proceed?" Judge Emhoff rumbled in his gruff voice without further pleasantries or preamble.

Martin's attorney is Kristie Calwis, a partner in the prominent firm of Tatterman, Keller and Toft. She's 40 years old and already twice divorced. My opinion of her, mostly formed from seeing her on television commercials, is that she tends to sound abrasive and shrill when speaking. Most attorneys know sounding shrill is simply not a good thing. I don't know why Martin hired Calwis for a criminal matter, because she is a divorce and family law lawyer.

My contacts opined that Calwis is definitely not an effective negotiator because she never thinks about first acquiring leverage or about what would appear reasonable. My past experience when dabbling in extracurricular legal matters for friends and acquaintances is that a large portion of the family and divorce attorneys never developed the skills needed to be effective negotiators because they simply default to demanding everything as they know the judge will eventually sort it out for them. That approach to law practice also tends to dramatically drive up the clients' costs, giving family law attorneys even more reason to continue on as they always have.

"Good morning, Judge Emhoff. For the record, I would like to restate our motion for a continuance based on the deaths of …" Calwis was saying when Judge Emhoff cut her off.

"Denied. Proceed with your hearing, Ms. Calwis."

Nonplussed, Calwis continued. "Your Honor, we think it is prejudicial to our client's position not to have sufficient time to prepare the arguments and ex—" she was saying when the judge interrupted again.

"Attorney Calwis, earlier this morning you were completely unable to articulate how their untimely deaths would affect the presentation or interpretation of evidence in this courtroom. Your petition for continuance is denied, and we will proceed with your hearing or the petition will be denied. Up to you."

Exchanging confused glances with Archer, I was shocked Judge Emhoff wouldn't even let Calwis make her record supporting their motion for continuance. Calwis hadn't done anything to piss off Emhoff that I was aware of, and it seemed like he just didn't want her to get the motion or arguments on the record.

To her credit, Calwis kept her composure in the face of Emhoff's judicial hostility. She briefly summarized the heart of the motion and then called the first witness. That was one of the reasons why Annabelle, Archer and I were here today.

"We call Jacob Archer to the stand."

After he was sworn in and Calwis had elicited a lengthy summary of his long experience as a detective in Prior Lake, Minnesota, Calwis could finally start asking Archer meaningful questions because his credibility had been established.

"Mr. Archer, please tell the court what you witnessed the night of July 30th of this year," Calwis asked.

Archer looked attentive but comfortable while he sat on the witness stand. He had done it more times than he could count during his decades on the job. "The night of July 30th, myself and Annabelle Masterson were reviewing the security of Terry Triton's lake cottage near the Boundary Waters when we detected an intruder into the main structure late in the evening. We entered the structure and discovered Samantha Triton standing in front of Terry Triton, who was seated. She was pointing a gun at him."

"Did you overhear them saying anything?" Calwis prompted. It was a leading question, but not one that anyone would object to in this hearing.

"Yes, we did. And our security cameras inside the building recorded the encounter," Archer clarified. His statement was meant to give Calwis a natural opportunity to introduce the security footage, using Archer as the person to authenticate the video.

Looking intrigued, Judge Emhoff allowed the video into evidence, which was marked as Exhibit 1 for the record. "Please proceed, Ms. Calwis."

Calwis nodded towards Archer, so he took the hint and began his narration. "This video excerpt was recorded at approximately 10:35 p.m. in the great room of Mr. Triton's cottage. On it you can clearly see and hear both Terry Triton and Samantha Triton as follows."

EXHIBIT 1 REPLAY

[Samantha Triton] I brought a beverage that you should enjoy. [Samantha Triton emerges from the darkness of the room. In her left hand she held a small beverage container, and in her right hand she held a small caliber pistol, pointed at Terry Triton.]

[Terry Triton] Thought you might show up. What's in the cup?"

[Samantha] Hemlock tea. It's for you.

[Terry] Or what? You'll shoot? Was that the choice you gave Bill Harrison, too?

[Samantha] Didn't have to point a gun at him. Bill thought he was sharing a cup of ordinary tea with his stooge, Erik, while they sat in his study and plotted to take down our company. Those fools had no idea they were about to

become corpses. Why am I bothering to tell you? I can see the question in your eyes.

[Terry] (nodding) The question did cross my mind, yes. I suppose it's because you feel a little confession is good for the soul?

[Samantha] Perhaps. Won't matter once you're gone. Make your choice, I can deal with you either way.

[Terry] (smiling broadly) Nah, I'm fine as is. We don't think you're in any position to call the shots now.

[Samantha's head tilted slightly to the right.] We? Who's we?

[Terry] Me. And them. (Terry points past Samantha with his chin.)

VIDEO ENDS

"Mr. Archer, how did you interpret Samantha Triton's statements in the video?" Calwis asked. She was standing right in front of the witness chair as she put the question to Archer.

Looking straight at Calwis, Archer responded, "My interpretation of Mrs. Triton's statements is that she was behind Mr. Harrison's death. The murder weapon may have actually been hemlock-laced tea, and Mr. Harrison's neck was broken only to hide the cause of death. It led the medical examiner to forego toxicology testing. Poisoning also would be, in my experience, a more likely cause of death given that Martin Triton's medical issues would have made it very difficult for him to actually break someone's neck."

"How so?" prompted Calwis. She appeared very interested in Archer's testimony.

"Mr. Triton is a 68-year old man who walks with a cane that he holds in his right hand. He has significant pain and weakness in his left hand from a bone chip injury to the left wrist. The autopsy of Mr. Harrison failed to note any signs of left side weakness in the choking of Harrison that led to his broken neck, and in the real world, it takes nearly super-human strength to snap a man's neck, so signs of left-handed weakness is evidence that Martin Triton didn't do it," Archer noted.

Calwis followed up with a few more questions before completing her direct exam of Archer. The prosecutor stood to take her turn with him on cross.

I hadn't researched anything about her prior to the hearing because that was Calwis' job, but I could observe that the prosecutor was in her early 30s, and had dark brown hair and bright blue eyes. Despite being tallish at around 5 feet, 8 inches, she was somewhat heavyset but obviously kept in shape by working out. Judging from the size of her shoulders, those workouts could have been anything from distance swimming to bench pressing riding lawn mowers.

"Mr. Archer, my name is Ann Morris. Thank you for your diligent work investigating the tragic murder of Bill Harrison and Martin Triton's conviction for that murder. The State also wishes to express our sympathy for last night's untimely death of Samantha Triton," Morris said.

I couldn't help but notice Morris' deep alto speaking voice and my vivid imagination had little trouble picturing her in a silky robe. No, not *that* kind of robe. I mean the kind of robe a gal with a voice like that would wear when singing in a choir. I lowered my eyes and softly muttered "Aw, dammit."

Annabelle looked sharply at me, as did Terry Triton and Calwis. I must have said it louder than I intended, so I whispered to Annabelle, "She's smooth. That's gonna be a problem."

It was definitely a problem. Calwis had not been able to convince a judge, any judge, to grant permission to exhume Harrison's corpse so it could be tested for hemlock or any other form of poisoning. Absent overwhelmingly convincing evidence, no judge was willing to disturb

Harrison's place of rest just because a truth-compromised inmate made allusions and insinuations regarding the death of a prominent and wealthy citizen. It was a glaring hole in Calwis' case that we had agreed would tilt the evidentiary scales of Triton's conviction to continue favoring the government. Morris had no difficulty discerning the weakness and exploiting it.

"Mr. Archer, if you could, can you tell the Court about Samantha Triton's confession to the killing of Bill Harrison?" asked Morris. Like any experienced, competent attorney, Morris knew the only possible answer to the question before she ever asked it of Archer.

While Archer was prepped to expect this question, there wasn't any way he could spin it in Triton's favor so he simply responded, "There wasn't an explicit confession by Mrs. Triton that I'm aware of."

Morris pressed the rhetorical knife further into the open wound. "Thank you, Mr. Archer. The State agrees that there was no confession." Morris turned to face Judge Emhoff before speaking again. "No more questions, your Honor."

I traded looks with Annabelle. She knew as well as I did that Morris was using brevity very effectively in this setting to weaken Martin's case by denying him a forum for his representatives to further articulate their case.

Within an hour, the hearing was over, and the motion was denied. Terry Triton joined Archer, Annabelle and myself at Forty-Three Gallons of Whiskey Brewing in Minnetonka to discuss the hearing over some cold brews. It was mid-afternoon on a weekday, so the crowd was sparse at the moment.

"Happened so fast, it almost makes your head spin," grumbled Triton before pausing to sip a Pro Foama. The fresh pour had left a thin layer of white foam atop the thick, dark beer. Despite Triton's dejected mood, his eyebrow rose in appreciation of the delicious flavor of the brew. "I guess that's it then. The murderers are dead, and we took our best shot at getting Dad out of jail. Now he's stuck and we got nothing."

Sipping his own Pro Foama, Archer grunted in agreement. "Getting kneecapped by the lack of corroborating evidence was definitely an Achilles' heel in there today. The judicial stonewalling over exhuming Harrison's body is going to continue now that the ladies are dead."

Annabelle chuffed slightly. "Ryan going rabbit to God knows where now means that's it. We've got nothing more to run with. Investigation is over. I'm going to start updating the footnotes to the Trifecta of Terror links on the show's website with the details from today's hearing. Beyond that, I have no idea what to do." Ironically, Annabelle's beer of choice today was a hazy IPA called Capital Offense. She apparently was drowning her sorrows because she already was on her second pint.

Saying nothing, I merely sipped my bourbon, which was named Amicus Curiae, and savored the rich, caramel taste and smooth finish. After a beat down like today, even though we had expected it, the gang needed to drink heavily and blow off steam. It wasn't hard to see that calling up a couple of rideshare drivers was in tonight's plans.

CHAPTER 13

The buzzing of the phone on the nightstand awakened me. Bleary-eyed, I rolled over and fumbled for the damn thing and it clattered back to the top of the nightstand before I finally got a hold of it. "Hello?" I finally asked, hoping I was now awake enough to sound coherent despite having been in a deep sleep.

"Good morning, Sunshine. It's a beautiful morning out there. The sun is shining. The clouds are wispy. And—" Annabelle was saying when I interrupted her.

"You know, I could always kill you and make another who looks just like you," I grumbled. I was pretty hopeful the words that tumbled out were in English, but without coffee, all bets were off that my brain wasn't just mumbling in a fog again.

"... And the birds are singing beautiful music. Just like in the last recordings of Samantha Triton," Annabelle continued, completely unfazed by my mock threat. She and her siblings had heard that old joke about making another to replace them since they were little.

Now I was even more confused. "What recordings?"

"From the bugs that Joel planted in Samantha Triton's study," Annabelle said quickly. She was excited about something, but the dots weren't connecting yet.

"Start at the beginning and walk me through it," I said, sitting up in bed. The fog of deep sleep finally started to lift.

"OK. Yesterday, I was working up the final show notes to wrap up our Trifecta of Terror reporting for the Harrison and Johnson murders when I noticed the surveillance bugs that Joel planted continued to auto-record even though we had stopped listening to them after we had captured the conversation where Samantha and Tammy were discussing killing off Ryan. There were a bunch of recordings, so I fed them into the system and had an AI index and summarize the recordings to make reviewing them quicker."

Mentioning AI summaries of bugged secret conversations of a dead woman caught my full attention, just like she knew it would. "Um, so you're saying there's more incriminating stuff in those recordings?" I asked.

Annabelle chuffed softly. "Oh, yeah. Some real gems in there. Enough, I hope, to allow Martin to go forward with a renewed motion based on new evidence."

"Couldn't hurt. But Martin fired Calwis after the hearing blew up. He finally realized we were right that her experience wasn't a good fit with the type of story he needs to bring before the Court."

Sighing in exasperation, Annabelle had to agree. "Alright, yeah. You told me the 'Right Tools Right Job' rule applies just as much to mechanics as it does to doctors and lawyers. Get the right tools into the hands that have the right experience."

Snorting, I could only approve that my daughter still remembered that piece of advice. You never know whether your fatherly pronouncements go in one ear and out the other, or somehow manage to stick. "Exactly. You shouldn't send a lawn mower mechanic to fix a 747 any more than you should send a bankruptcy attorney to litigate a shareholder derivatives class action. Can you package up everything you've got, including the summaries, and make them available to Tavington? I need to call him anyway, and I could give him a heads up about what all the data is about."

"Will do. Can't wait to hear what he's got to say about it," Annabelle remarked, then she ended the call.

I tumbled out of bed and got started getting cleaned up for the day before making a call to Jerry. I needed some time to wake up and mull over what Annabelle had said. As I was finishing up with shaving, something clicked in my head. It was time to make the call.

Tavington picked up after the second ring. "What's up?"

"We need to do some thinking and drinking."

Barking a laugh, Tavington said, "My favorite kind of thinking. How'd you know?"

"Well, we have some new data to go over about Martin's case. Annabelle is sending you the data links so you can check it all out. Seeing how Martin's last hearing didn't go swimmingly ..." I was saying when Tavington interrupted with a laugh.

"To say the least!"

I continued. "Can you take a listen to what we've got now? Look over the AI transcript summaries. They are additional recordings that our surveillance bugs continued to make after we stopped listening."

"Really?" Tavington said, his voice betraying his rising interest. "Of our favorite leading lady?"

"The one and only. Obviously, Martin got jobbed during his last hearing because all they had was some secondhand hearsay as circumstantial evidence of his innocence. Now that he's gone down in flames, my thinking is he's going to want to gear up for a new motion using this evidence. Problem is, I'm not too sure how strong it is as I need to give a listen to those calls myself," I summarized for Tavington.

"And you suspect it won't be enough to push the motion over the finish line now that the first hearing died a harsh death," Tavington said. He succinctly stated the feeling gnawing at my gut over the strength of the new evidence.

"Correct in one. Plus, this particular evidence would have to fit the hearsay exemptions. Like being an utterance against interest by a declarant who is no longer available, or an excited utterance, or something," I said. "Whatever the State versions of Federal Rules 803 and 804 are, as I recall."

"Oooh, baby! I love it when you talk dirty to me. Let's meet tomorrow late afternoon. My office.

"See you then."

The next afternoon came round quickly. It was a perfect early fall day, with temps hovering near the mid-50s. Many trees had shed their leaves by now, although there were still die-hard maples and lindens stubbornly clinging to their leaves. I enjoyed the view on the short drive over to Tavington's office and arrived soon after his last clients of the day departed along with his staff.

"What's your poison?" Tavington asked when I walked into the firm's staff-only conference room unannounced. He was at the wet bar and was thinking of making a bourbon, neat. Tavington and I both tended to prefer a 100% corn-based bourbon made in South Carolina from a heritage strain of red corn kernels. It was very good stuff. Neither of us cared for more wheated bourbons — they reminded us too much of rubbing alcohol.

Today, however, I wasn't in the mood for bourbon. "Brandy Old Fashioned."

Tavington looked up at me in surprise because he knew what ordering that particular drink meant. Both of us had spent a lot of time in Wisconsin, where the brandy version of an Old Fashioned was more popular than the whisky version, and we had become enamored of it. We crafted our own version of the cocktail with an apple brandy that has a touch of cinnamon, mixed with sour cherry, orange crema, Demerara syrup, Angostura bitters, Sprite, bourbon cherries, and a twist of sliced orange. Brandy Old Fashioned was our comfort drink when we needed one. Putting the unpoured bourbon away, Tavington began mixing up several brandy Old Fashioneds.

"What did you think of those recordings?" Tavington asked as he handed me a glass.

Sipping the Old Fashioned, I replied, "Good, but not great."

Looking confused, Tavington asked, "The drink? Or the recordings?"

"Recordings. It's pretty decent evidence that Martin didn't kill anybody, but without Samantha Triton to authenticate the statements, just trying to introduce that evidence will trigger a festival of objections by the State."

Tavington nodded and put his feet up on the table as he leaned way back into his seat. "Agreed. Due to the failure of the original motion, we're already swimming upstream …" he was saying when I interrupted.

"We're? Who's "we're"?"

Half-smiling now, Tavington answered the question. "Martin hired me an hour ago to try to get a new motion underway."

Eyebrows rising in surprise, I just looked at Tavington and didn't know what to say.

CHAPTER 14

OCTOBER 1

MOBILE HOME PARK – SHAKOPEE, MINNESOTA

The setting of the early October sun illuminated Annabelle's flaming red hair and enhanced her naturally blonde highlights to spectacular effect as she walked up the steps with Jerry Tavington to the small porch near the front door of the well maintained, double-wide trailer home. Trading looks with Tavington, Annabelle then knocked on the door.

A woman in her early 60s answered the knock. She had shoulder-length graying hair that retained some of its original auburn, and large brown eyes.

"Yes? Can I help you?" the woman asked. She looked both confused and a bit concerned at seeing Annabelle and Tavington on her porch.

"Mrs. Johnson? I'm Annabelle Masterson, and this is my associate, Jerry Tavington. May we have a few minutes of your time?"

Mrs. Johnson's face hardened with a brief flash of annoyance. "I'm sorry, I'm in the middle of cooking some dinner after my shift. Whatever you're selling, I can assure you I don't have the money for it." While she said this, Donna Johnson looked them over as if trying to figure out why they looked vaguely familiar.

Getting the brush off for appearing to be selling vacuums door-to-door caused Tavington to raise his eyebrows slightly and a sardonic smile crept onto his face. "No, ma'am. We're not salespeople nor are we here to save your soul. I'm an attorney and Annabelle is—" he began stating when recognition suddenly dawned across Donna Johnson's visage.

"You're the 'Murder in Minnesota' people!" Mrs. Johnson interrupted excitedly.

Annabelle nodded. "Yes, ma'am. We were wondering if you'd speak with us about an investigation we've been pursuing."

Annabelle was secretly pleased that Mrs. Johnson was familiar with the show and who they were. From her research, Annabelle knew that Mrs. Johnson worked long hours as a fabrication machine operator in a factory making lawn care equipment and spent additional time advancing the membership of her branch of the local union. Annabelle would have bet that Mrs. Johnson just didn't have the spare time to keep up with "Murder in Minnesota." She was delighted to be wrong about her assumption.

Looking confused and suspicious, Mrs. Johnson asked, "Is this about my son? If you're going to try to pin any murders on him, count me out."

It was Annabelle's turn to look surprised, and she shook her head. "Only tangentially about him. We think your son was a victim, not a perpetrator."

Now it was Mrs. Johnson's turn to look surprised, but the look passed quickly. "Well then, now you're preaching to the choir. Why don't you two come in and I'll make us some coffee."

After they were settled around the dining table, both Annabelle and Tavington realized that Mrs. Johnson had simply turned off the burners on the stove top with the ingredients for her dinner still in the pans.

The half-cooked food turned cold and dry during their long discussion.

* * *

"What are we looking for?" Archer asked as he mouse clicked through search options on the screen in front of him.

Terry Triton and I traded glances and we both shrugged in unison. Each of us was seated in front of different laptops set up in Terry's office at Triton Industries. "That's the problem. We don't know, exactly. Annabelle and Tavington are working the angles with Erik Johnson's mother to try to dig up some direct evidence of foul play. We're on a fishing expedition to see if something looks amiss in the data records of a large, multinational corporation," I wryly stated about our predicament.

Archer stopped what he was doing and looked up at me. "Helpful." He shook his head and grumbled. "Like looking for one particular needle in a haystack of needles."

I snorted. "Probably every bit as futile as polishing Hindenburg's silverware before landing in Lakehurst." I cleared my throat before continuing. "What I'm thinking is we focus on the 'Why.' Specifically, why have *all* these corpses that turned up. Then search and see if there's any company data that might tell us why they're dead."

Terry sat back in his seat and mulled over the implications of what I just said. "That means we're looking for more than just who killed Harrison."

"We already know your dead stepmom killed Harrison and Johnson in her bid to take over the company. We know that your dad schemed to destroy Harrison's business and that he was framed for Harrison's death. We also know that your stepmom was involved in a love triangle with two people, one of whom is dead and the other mostly missing. So, using Dante's logic about searching for a 'Why,' we need to figure out why Samantha and Tammy are dead and who did it," Archer reported, concisely summing up the messy state of the investigation so far.

I added, "That gives us two angles to run down, which may be connected beyond the love triangle. Or maybe not. Tammy "The Sex Kitten" Kettle enjoyed her drugs and colorful interactions with younger men down at Sorvino's speakeasy, but Sorvino told me he's not aware of her having any transactions or schemes beyond enthusiastically being a drugged-up cougar. Sorvino also said if Tammy was trying to use any of her trysts to blackmail other lovers, he hasn't caught wind of it because that sort of thing is pretty intimate and there normally wasn't opportunity to capture it on film or audio except for our last trip down there to watch the series finale of the Tammy Kettle Show."

Nodding, Terry seemed to agree with where I was going with this line of reasoning. "So, we focus on finding connections with Samantha, not Tammy, because Tammy's extracurricular festivities aren't likely to cause a third party to kill off my stepmother as well."

"That's right," Archer said. "Unless we stumble across something linking Tammy's hanky-panky with Samantha beyond their threesome with Ryan, I think we have better odds of uncovering something pertaining to Samantha."

"Since the source of Samantha's power and influence derives from Triton Industries, here we are," Terry concluded. "OK. It's 8:30 Saturday morning, so we have all weekend. Let's see what we dig up."

Hours passed. The sun crept across the sky and eventually set unheeded. Leaning back into my seat, I finally noticed Archer remained hunched over his laptop while Terry kept inputting new searches. I leaned further back and put my feet up on the top of the table I was sitting at. Glancing down at my yellow pad, the blank yellow page seemed like a beacon calling attention to the utter futility of the past 10 hours. I shook my head and quietly sighed in frustration.

"The sigh of failure?" Archer asked, looking over his laptop screen. His face looked tired. So did Terry's, so it wasn't hard to imagine that mine mirrored theirs.

"Crashed and burned. I can't find anything useful in Triton's records pertaining to Samantha," I groused.

Terry nodded. "Yeah. I triple checked her actions on the board or on behalf of the company, and nothing struck a chord with me. I couldn't even imagine how any of it would have impacted someone enough to motivate them to break into the jail and take her out."

Leaning back into his seat with hands clasped behind his head, Archer just shook his head as he looked towards the ceiling. "At this point, I'm thinking her corporate life with Triton Industries doesn't give me reason to think anyone should be implicated in ending her. So, what are we missing?"

I was thunderstruck with an insight from Archer's words. "Her corporate life with Triton Industries?"

Before I could continue, Terry added, "None of it seems particularly controversial."

"What if we're looking into the wrong collection of corporate records?" I asked sharply. The distinction Archer accidentally made was still boomeranging around my head. That distinction carried numerous implications.

Confusion spread across Terry and Archer's faces because I hadn't explained what I was now thinking yet. "There's other records?" Archer asked quizzically.

I held up my left index finger to indicate "wait a minute" and sorted out my thoughts before speaking. "What if we're looking at this all wrong? Instead of Samantha's actions being the cause of her demise, maybe we should be looking at this as if her demise was about someone else's actions?"

For a few moments, both of them looked at me as if I were mad, then understanding dawned on them simultaneously. "Martin," Archer concluded, then traded glances with Terry.

"We need to look at records pertaining to Martin," Terry said aloud, articulating what we were all thinking.

My cell rang. I saw it was Heidi so naturally I answered it. "Hey, Papa! Don't forget we're taking care of Mary and Emily tonight," Heidi said.

I glanced at my watch to confirm the dinner hour was fast approaching. "Yep. We're going to wrap up here and I'll be there in about a half hour. The girls there yet?" Even though they could only hear my side of the call, Archer and Terry took that as their cue to call it a day and began gathering their things.

"You'll get here about shortly after they arrive. See you in a bit," Heidi said before we ended the call.

"Same bat time and same bat cave tomorrow?" Archer inquired.

I nodded. "It's a date. Maybe we'll find something then."

By the time I arrived home, the house was filled with all of my girls. It was time to settle down, sit on the floor with my granddaughters and play with them because that is Papa's "Job # 1" as far as I'm concerned.

* * *

"We have to follow the money. That always leads to the truth," Archer said the next morning as he poured the first of many cups of coffee that day. We were back in Terry's office bright and early, and the three of us decided to talk about yesterday first.

I chuffed a small laugh. "Like you read my mind."

"That's creepy. I've seen the sort you hang out with," Archer noted dryly. "Ain't nobody want to get between your ears."

"I'm thinking there will basically be three types of financial records we can look at," Terry stated. "Investments, reimbursements and disbursements."

"What's the difference between reimbursements and disbursements?" Archer asked. "Aren't they basically the same thing?"

"Well, yes and no. Yes, because both involve funds leaving company coffers. No, because It depends upon which account the funds are drawn from and the purpose for the draw," Terry said before taking a quick sip of his coffee.

"That was almost helpful," Archer quipped. "Any more insights you can give?"

"Reimbursements, at least here, generally means reimbursing employees for work-related expenses. Personal licenses for our attorneys, flights, that sort of thing. Disbursements are for direct corporate purchases. The cars for our sales force. Raw materials we can turn into munitions. Parts for weapons," Terry added.

I couldn't help but note that Terry spoke about weapons manufacturing as if it were any other product. Like it wasn't anything more interesting than making a garden tractor or shovels. Maybe it was just me being cynical, but it seems like making products that go 'boom' ought to be somewhat more fascinating. Obviously, talking about explosions was more exciting than simply making the ordnance but for some reason I expected more energy in his description.

"So, we start by looking for outliers in the financial data. Look at the extremes and where that takes us," Terry said. "Dante, you take investments. Archer, can you look through the reimbursements? I'll take disbursements."

"Erm. You boys realize I'm just a humble attorney, right?" I asked, causing them both to chuckle.

"*You*?" Archer asked without bothering to try to mask his sarcasm even slightly. "Have you looked up the meaning of 'humble' before?"

"My mathematical skills are limited to counting fingers and toes." I got the feeling neither of these guys realized the sad, truncated extent of my math skills.

"Bullshit. You went through law school." Archer countered. He was looking at me like I was a child trying to get out of shoveling snow off the driveway.

"Hey, the old joke that lawyers are wannabe doctors who couldn't do math and went to law school instead isn't a common joke among law students for no reason. Fair warning here that my modest math skills are much to be modest about."

"Yeah, but you're a lawyer and all those numbers have dollar signs. You'll be fine," Archer assured me.

"I hate you," I said.

"I know," Archer responded. The broad smile he wore was the most malicious one he could muster.

Unfortunately, our banter turned out to be the most productive activity we engaged in throughout the day. Night had again fallen before we completed our review of the company's financial records. The three of us gathered around the meeting table in Terry's office, exhaustion plainly evident in our faces. Terry stood up, stretched, and turned to the cabinet behind his seat and opened it.

"We need thinking juice," Terry said, as he poured three glasses of bourbon, neat, and passed them around.

"I like where you're going with this," I quipped as Terry handed me a glass with several fingers of caramel-colored booze in it.

Terry and Archer took sips and Archer sighed. "Ahh. Neat. Just as God intended bourbon to be," he said in satisfaction before continuing. "I found bupkis in reimbursements. Few recurring reimbursements, and none of those added up to sufficient motivation to assassinate the ladies."

"Disbursements are all over the place, so I have a couple dozen payees to have our accountants investigate and report about. I just want to confirm those payees are above board. Beyond that, as far as I could tell, the ledger is clean," Terry concluded. He took another sip of the bourbon and tilted his head back and rubbed his eyes.

"I found the killers," I said simply.

Heads snapped back to stare intently at me. "What? Why didn't you tell us earlier?" Archer asked before he suddenly looked at me suspiciously.

"No, of course I didn't. That's what you get for making me dig through investment records all damn day," I grumbled. "Like Terry, I have some things to follow up on. There's lots of big holdings by investment firms, plus decent sized holdings by small investors hidden behind corporate facades of various types. LLCs, partnerships, things like that. But there's one thing that bothered me from a high-level point of view. We're only looking at half of the data." I was looking at Terry when I finished my report.

Understanding suddenly dawned on Terry's face as he processed my words. He clearly hadn't thought of this aspect. "The acquisition of Harrison's company!" he suddenly exclaimed. Terry was getting excited now. "Harrison's data hasn't been integrated into ours because the Defense

Department requires us to keep it separate for antitrust purposes! Dammit! Why didn't I see that before?"

Hours of researching this new angle passed, and the bourbon was getting pretty low in the decanter by the time I called out, "Hey. Take a look at these lists I've got side-by-side on my screen."

Archer and Terry wandered over to stand behind me. "What are we looking at?" Archer asked.

I pressed a button and highlighted several rows in yellow on the spreadsheet. "Recall that Harrison's company took a bath by being fed false data through Johnson? I got three data sets to show you. These are the institutional investors that also invested in Triton Industries, highlighted in yellow."

"Yeah? Soooo …" Archer said, drawing out the last word in an effort to get me to connect the dots for them a little faster since it was late in the evening now and we were boozing our way into the night.

I removed the yellow highlights and highlighted some other rows in blue. "Second set. These investors lost money in Harrison's company when the stock tanked. Again, all large institutional investment houses. There really weren't too many individual investors that caught my attention because the financial stakes weren't large, so I did not include them here. Neither sets one nor two tell us anything particularly significant, unlike the third set."

I then removed the blue highlights and highlighted a set of rows in pale red. "This is the third set. Short sellers. This group made money betting against Harrison's company by borrowing a broker's shares of stock in Harrison's company, then selling those shares just before the price tanked. This group of investors subsequently bought back replacement shares at the lower price and returned them to the broker to extinguish their loan. These particular investors then kept the 'borrow and sell high, buyback low' price differential as their profit. There are only four of them. Notice the investment institution at the bottom of the list."

Both men peered intently to read the text. Terry answered first. "A union?"

Archer gruffly added more clarification for Terry since Archer recognized the entity. "It's Local 28240-A. Some sort of newer union of county-level supervisory personnel and a few others. They claim to have all these members, but no one has ever been able to verify those claims."

"How many supervisory personnel can there possibly be?" Terry asked. "Wouldn't that be a rather small number?"

"Not only would it realistically have a small number of members, this little union nonetheless had enough money to make millions by a massive short selling scheme. Once Triton Industries acquired Harrison's company and replaced those stocks with Triton Industries stock, the short selling activity of Harrison's company would basically have been laundered. Superficially, these numbers seem way off to me."

Archer glanced at me. "Still doesn't mean the union had anything to do with ending Tammy or Samantha."

"Nope. But what if the guards on duty during Samantha's demise were members of Local 28240-A?" I asked.

"Then that would be one helluva coincidence," Archer concluded.

"Thought you don't believe in coincidences," I said. It was a statement, not a question.

Archer raised one eyebrow in agreement. "I don't."

CHAPTER 15

"**S**pecial delivery," Heidi said as she handed me an envelope from her short trip to the mailbox on the corner leading into our little cul-de-sac. She kissed me on top of my forehead as she passed by the front office on her way to the kitchen to grab some breakfast. "It was on the front porch," she called over her shoulder.

Still sitting in my chair, I looked at the envelope. It was addressed to me, and had no return address. "Gotta be my Mysterious Friend," I mumbled absently and tore the envelope open. Inside was a slip of paper bearing the expected message consisting entirely of an unrecognized phone number. I stood up and quickly closed the pocket doors to my office, then called the number from my backup burner phone. It was answered after the first ring. "This is Dante," I said by way of introduction.

"My friend, it is good to hear from you. I am pleased that you have made the acquaintance of a good friend of mine," said the now-familiar voice of my Mysterious Friend. "He speaks highly of you."

I had to smile at that. "We got along very well, thank you. You know some interesting people."

"Sí. I have another friend I would like you to visit. I will tell you about her. This will not be a difficult visit for you this time," Mysterious Friend promised.

I scribbled down the instructions on a notepad from my desk drawer. This visit didn't sound all that exciting, but I'd do it anyway because crossing swords with my Mysterious Friend is a hazardous proposition. Once he finished passing along his instructions, the conversation turned to other topics.

"This is good, my friend. Do you need anything up there?" he asked.

"Um. Actually, can I bend your ear for a minute? We're about to investigate something up here for 'Murder in Minnesota' and I want to make sure we don't accidentally step on your toes," I said diplomatically.

"It is wise to check with me. What are you going to do? Is it a new murder investigation, or one you've been working on for a while?" he asked.

The familiar manner of his questions startled me a little bit so I answered his question with a question. "Have you been following along with the show?" I asked.

"Of course! We have become … loyal followers ever since the false prosecution of your daughter by Keisha Lewiston. My men gossip like old women after each episode." His Hispanic accent only accentuated the depth of meaning he meant to convey.

Mysterious Friend being this familiar with "Murder in Minnesota" was definitely *not* a direction I had anticipated the conversation going. "Oh! Didn't realize you guys followed the show. We're still working the investigation around Martin Triton, the billionaire industrialist and the recent murder of his wife, Samantha, while she was in jail."

"Her guards were dirty," Mysterious Friend interjected. He sounded certain, and obviously had been listening to the episodes we had streamed.

"Yeah. We think so too, but we now think it's time to follow the money to find out *why* a union for county-level supervisory personnel may have wanted her gone. We think it involves a possible short selling scheme by the union, which then iced her to hide the union's involvement," I summarized. Even as I said it, the theory sounded full of holes but it was the only partially developed theory I could offer up at the moment. So far, it hadn't even risen to the level of being plausible.

There was a moment's pause before he asked, "How do you intend to investigate this union?"

That was the million-dollar question. I had to be honest because my Mysterious Friend had proven himself to be quite perceptive and adept at spotting deception. "I wish I knew, because we haven't figured that out yet. Short of breaking in at night and copying their books, we got nothing."

Mysterious Friend then said, "You're looking into Local 28240-A. It is a very dangerous enemy. If you don't destroy it entirely, they'll make an example of you. And your family."

"How did you know which union?" I asked.

"I know them. They need to pay their debts," he said cryptically. A few moments passed before Mysterious Friend then added, "Do nothing to investigate them until I say you can. You will hear from me in a few days."

There was nothing more to discuss, so I agreed to wait since I had no other choice, and we finished up the call. I had no idea if Mysterious Friend had some sort of relationship with that union and I didn't really want to find out. Too bad the choice had just been taken out of my hands.

I immediately called Archer on my regular cell phone.

"You got an idea?" Archer said as his way of answering the call.

"Yes and no. I checked with my source, who instructed me to wait a couple days to hear from him. He confirmed the union is a dangerous operator in the way we suspected," I informed him.

"Your source say what he's gonna do?" Archer asked.

"No. My guess is he'll pass along whatever relevant info he obtains about the union. I don't know. But he's also not someone to ignore."

Archer's cynical snort of disbelief said more than what he articulated. "Unvetted, anonymous sources telling you to trust them? That's like trusting porn site ads for meeting singles."

"This source has come through for us before. And your familiarity with sketchy porn ads concerns me," I replied. "Your browser history must really be something."

"Don't forget you're supposed to wipe my browser history if something happens to me," Archer quipped. "So, what do we do in the meantime?"

"I guess we'll just sit tight on the Triton investigation. For now, Tavington is drafting a Petition for Disinterment for Mr. Johnson so he can file it and get it on the court docket. If this source follows his previous pattern, we won't have to wait very long," I said. "I guess you'll have to learn how to color with crayons or something until then."

"You mean, like, coloring inside the lines? Ain't happening," Archer said dryly. "Alright, gives me time to get some projects done around the house. We still grilling salmon over at your place tonight?"

"Yep. With olive oil, crushed garlic and pepper, just the way you like it. Bring wine," I said.

* * *

Four days later, my latest burner phone rang. It was an unfamiliar, unlisted number, so naturally, I answered the call. "Hello?"

The Hispanic accent was immediately recognizable. "Hello, my friend. I have that information you wanted. Tomorrow night, the cleaning person can get you into the hall that you wanted to look into. He will discover a broken water pipe and make an emergency call for the plumbers. The alarm system will then be deactivated for the plumbers to get inside. Is this acceptable?"

I was stunned, because it appeared our Mysterious Friend had taken seriously my halfway random thought about "breaking in at night and copying their books." Much more seriously than I had, because I had mostly forgotten about it. Breaking into a shady union's hall wasn't the best idea in the world, but if it weren't for bad ideas, we wouldn't have any ideas at all right now.

"We'll be there. Anything you want us to look for?" I asked.

"Copies of any records you find," Mysterious Friend said. "I would enjoy looking at those."

I smiled savagely. "With pleasure. Can you keep those from getting loose in the wild until after we make use of them for the show?" I asked. It was a big ask since the guy was rigging it so we could break into places better left alone.

"Of course. I will enjoy hearing your show's opinion about the records, but we will never let anyone know we have them until after they are in the news. My associate will text you further instructions."

The short call ended. I realized we needed all hands on deck for this excursion to make it seem somewhat believable. After notifying Annabelle and Archer, I called my son.

"Hey, Dad, what's up?" Joel asked by way of answering the call.

"I need to borrow you for the show tomorrow night," I said.

"You had me at sneaky and underhanded," Joel quipped, because I hadn't suggested anything like that. Yet. I could already hear the interest in his voice.

"Our cover is we're posing as plumbers making an emergency visit. You got any tools to help with this?"

Joel snorted. "I know a guy. We can even use his van but we'll have to change the logo and license plates."

"Perfect. Further instructions to follow as we receive them." I ended the call and scrambled to start getting things ready.

The next evening arrived quickly and we gathered our incursion team together about a mile from the union hall. It was located in an office park in the eastern metro suburb of Woodbury. There were rows of similarly styled, multi-floor office buildings occupied by all sorts of companies. Bordering two sides of the complex of buildings were established upper middle-class neighborhoods, lined with numerous biking trails and parks for the residents. Archer and I pulled up next to Joel and my son-in-law Jeffrey sitting in a borrowed plumber's van. Windows rolled down in both rides.

"Plates?" Archer asked.

"Fake," replied Joel. "Our magnetic logo and artwork are fresh off the printer. Nice ride," Joel noted. "You steal it?"

"Tactically acquired," Archer said. "Actual owner just doesn't know it's gone. New plates, too."

My phone buzzed with an incoming text, which I read aloud for the group. "OK, it's go time. Alarm is off. The cleaner is waiting for our arrival. You and Jeffrey get in, copy their files, and get the hell out. We'll be lurking outside to keep watch. Your burner phones are on now?"

Archer, Joel and Jeffrey checked to confirm their phones were on, and we checked to make sure they were working. "If I send a message telling you guys to get out, drop what you're doing and leave. Don't ask why, just assume trouble is coming and it's time to be elsewhere," I said. "Let's do this."

Joel and Jeffrey drove directly to the union hall. Archer and I parked a couple blocks away, grabbed our gear and ran to separate buildings nearby. At this point I wasn't sure where Archer had decided to set up, so I climbed an exterior fire ladder to gain the roof of a building situated on a corner about a hundred yards from the union hall. It had a commanding view all around the area to the front of the building, but most importantly, I could watch the roads leading to the hall.

Texting, I sent "In position," while I watched Joel and Jeffrey through my rifle scope as they unloaded various plumbing tools from the van. It was chilly, and I could see their breath in the air. Jeffrey scratched his head, which was the prearranged signal to acknowledge the message was received. Both of them had gone so far with tonight's deception that they were wearing matching shirts emblazoned with the newly created logo on the side of the van and had temporarily dyed their hair blonde. It was startling to see Joel with a blonde beard. He looked like a Norse Viking.

I could see a cleaner was ushering Joel and Jeffrey inside. "Cleaning Guy," was built like a brick. About a foot shorter than Joel, and about as wide as both Joel and Jeffrey put together. He was so stacked, Cleaning Guy looked like he could break people in half for fun.

Despite the cold, we settled in to keep watch.

* * *

His face lit by the ghostly light from a computer screen, Joel called, "J, over here." They were using only the letter "J" to call out to one another to avoid using their actual names inside. Moments later, the two of them were looking at a listing of encrypted files on the screen.

"How'd you get in?" Jeffrey asked. He was curious how Joel could have hacked into the union hall's server so quickly.

With a point of his chin towards the far corner of the desk he was sitting at, Joel simply answered, "Our friend who let us in said I should try the manufacturer login on that slip of paper. It looks like whoever installed this system forgot to delete the original manufacturer's default backdoor credentials."

"They added their own, but forgot to delete the backdoor?" Jeffrey asked incredulously. He shook his head slightly in disbelief. "And here we got all geared up for nothing." Jeffrey was looking at the hacking gear they had just unpacked that was hidden inside their "plumbing" toolbox.

"Couple more minutes, then we can bolt," Joel said distractedly. His eyes were locked onto the screen as he navigated through the server. "This system isn't connected to the 'net. At all. And this PC has been hardwired for direct access. There are no other access points to the server." As he said this, Joel finished copying the files on the server and he quickly pocketed the thumb drive.

Frowning, Jeffrey asked, "So they have a standalone, encrypted server but left the default login backdoor? And the only access is through this PC? Something ain't right."

Seconds later, their radios came alive. "Company coming. Bail now." Archer's terse message caused the boys to finish up.

Jeffrey and Joel hurriedly grabbed their gear and made for the door. They had been careful not to disturb anything, and Joel had taken a few seconds to wipe down the PC he had used to remove any residual oils and fingerprints. As they scrambled into the borrowed plumbing van they heard rifle shots echoing through the office complex.

"Shit. Shit. Shit!" Joel said through clenched teeth as Jeffrey stomped on the gas pedal in panic. The van's tires squealed as they took off away from the union hall.

A black SUV whipped around the backside of the hall and jumped the curb to follow the plumbing van. Its engine roared and sparks patterned across the road when the SUV skidded to a stop as the unseen driver attempted to change directions to pursue the van. More rifle shots sounded across the office complex and the windshield of the SUV was holed multiple times by bullet impacts. Just as the driver regained control, additional bullets shattered the driver side window. At the same time, the tires on the passenger side were blown out by successive rifle shots originating from Archer.

The SUV stopped all motion and the driver side door swung open slightly before slamming shut and sending the remaining bits of shattered glass from the window flying throughout the interior so the window space was now cleared of debris. Whoever was still inside tried to remain below the bottom of the window opening as they fought to control the broken door and still drive. The driver gunned the engine and the SUV slowly pulled away from the union hall because the flat tires on the passenger side impeded faster acceleration. Smoke quickly filled the air as additional bullet strikes impacted the engine compartment from two sides, causing the engine to rapidly overheat and burn oil that was now dripping through the new holes in the engine. Our efforts at discouraging pursuit weren't effective enough to dissuade these guys from following the van.

That changed quickly when the SUV was abruptly stopped by the appearance of Cleaning Guy, who had initially opened the union hall for Jeffrey and Joel. As I peered through my rifle scope, I could see Cleaning Guy calmly stepped through the glass and steel front doors of the union hall and took aim with what initially appeared to be an oversized rifle. It was actually an RPG anti-tank grenade launcher. Originally based on the WWII-era German Panzerfaust, this evolved RPG had been standardized by the Soviet Army for decades and is used by the militaries of many different countries and terrorist organizations. Where Cleaning Guy got his paws on one I'll never know, but he unhesitatingly fired the RPG straight into the rear of the departing SUV from about 30 yards. The resulting explosion was a cataclysmic fireball that rained fiery pieces of former SUV for dozens of yards in every direction while flame angrily boiled into the sky and lit up buildings for several blocks. When the initial fire and smoke cleared, Cleaning Guy had disappeared.

With the sudden erasure of the unwelcome SUV visitors, we all had another problem because the shooting and pyrotechnics meant we were now on the clock and would only have minutes before the badges began arriving in force. A firefight culminating in a huge fireball from an RPG in the middle of a wealthy suburb will draw more law enforcement than we could shake a stick at, so it was time to bale out on this adventure.

* * *

"Where the hell are they?" Joel cried out.

"I dunno!" Jeffrey said in a panicky voice.

"What the hell was that explosion?" said Joel. His voice was just as panicky.

"I dunno!" Jeffrey shot back.

"Where's Dad and Archer?" Joel continued.

"I don't know!" said Jeffrey. "I don't know. I dunno anything right now!" yelled Jeffrey in exasperation.

Jeffrey's irritation brought Joel back from the edge of panic. He sat quietly to gather his thoughts while Jeffrey drove them east towards the nearest edge of the metro. After a few minutes passed, Joel had made a decision.

"OK. We continue as planned and hope they got out. Archer said we're to drive deep into the woods and change the signage on the van and put the original plates back on. Then we take the northern backwoods roads all the way back to my buddy's place in Maple Grove and drop the van off. Then we each go home from there," Joel concluded. "Regroup in the morning and see what news there is."

Jeffrey nodded silently. They had hours of driving ahead of them.

* * *

Hiding in the shrubbery and tall grass along the edge of the office complex, Archer opened a pouch containing a toxic brew of ghost pepper mixed with vinegar. His nose immediately wrinkled in disgust at the vile smelling concoction as he sprinkled the torn down parts of his rifle with it. Then he buried those pieces of unmarked rifle parts, and sprinkled the surrounding area with the remaining brew to keep scents masked for a few days. By then he figured the search for far flung pieces of evidence would have ended, and nothing would ever be found. Even if they were dug up, there wasn't anything to connect them to us; we had surreptitiously acquired them from an individual we had investigated last year who was subsequently locked up for the next few decades so he wouldn't miss them.

Somewhat surprised, Archer looked at the short message on his burner phone. "Site Two," he mumbled aloud as he began ghosting between shadows along the edge of the office complex as quickly as he could. Various emergency vehicles already started roaring into the office complex from seemingly every direction and their lights and sirens made the empty buildings seem positively lively. His problem now was getting out and going to the new secondary position.

While he made his way towards the nearby neighborhood, Archer was a bit perplexed and briefly wondered what had happened to Site One, which was simply the designation Archer had given the vehicle that we had "borrowed" to get us here. He had been counting on using Site One to egress from the vicinity, and we had only come up with a vague idea of a Site Two as a fail-safe we had not expected to need.

The answer to Archer's question thundered into existence when Site One suddenly exploded. The fireball it made wasn't as severe as the one from the RPG, yet Archer had no trouble figuring out it was our booby-trapped loaner that just blew up about a mile from his current position.

He checked his watch and was surprised that merely 7 minutes had elapsed since the initial firefight. Archer could hear the distant, rhythmic "whop" sound of a helicopter approaching the office complex in the chilly night air. "I gotta get the hell outta here," he grumbled, unused to the role of being the hunted instead of the hunter. Archer waited until the side street was clear for a few moments, discarded his burner phone in a smelly pond of standing water, and then stole across in the road's poorly lit shadows to enter the nearby residential neighborhood. Even though many of the residents were now outside trying to catch a glimpse of what was going on, none had caught sight of the former detective as he made his way through the darkest parts of their neighborhood.

He stopped briefly to quietly unwind and cut a length of rope from a boat trailer, then, on the next block, he leaned over a fence and encouraged a friendly seeming dog to come closer. Archer tied the rope around the body of the dog so it made a decent enough leash, and he set the pooch on the ground. "Beggars can't be choosers," he muttered to himself as he stood up. The dog was some sort of mutt, and didn't seem too bright either since it was happy enough to go for a walk with a stranger. Archer knew from his years of policing that law enforcement rarely bothered dog walkers, figuring such people were mostly likely just local residents minding their own business.

The deception worked, because neither police nor civilians paid him any attention while he walked with the dog several miles to get completely out of the neighborhood. Spotting a walking trail winding down into the inky blackness near a tree-lined park and lake, Archer said goodbye to his canine companion and released it back into the wild. He figured someone would find the dumb dog and return it to the owner's home listed on its dog tag. Walking down into the dark trail, Archer pulled a second burner phone from a pocket and turned it on for the first time.

The problem with Site Two wasn't so much that they needed a backup site to regroup at. It was that we hadn't picked out the location for Site Two in advance. As Archer hoped, there was a message already waiting in his inbox on the new phone. It was an address in St. Paul that was a bit over a mile away from his current position.

Half an hour later, a tired and cold Archer pushed through the doors of a little hole-in-the-wall dive bar to find me waiting for him. Cigarette smoke wafted through the air of this dimly lit establishment, and I used the hand holding my glass of bourbon to motion towards a couple more glasses of bourbon that were already waiting for Archer at our table. The drinks were neat, with no ice.

Pursing his lips and nodding his approval, Archer sat down and we clinked our glasses together. "What a night," Archer said solemnly, before taking a large sip of the caramel-colored booze. He sighed after the burn of the liquid hit his belly.

"Annabelle is on her way to pick us up, so we just stay here and drink for now," I said. There were various television sets on in the tavern, and several of them were showing live news reports from the fracas at the office complex. "Natural disasters and police don't bother old drunks in a bar," I added. I spoke quietly, letting the noise of the boisterous crowd cover the sound of my voice.

Archer snorted in approval. "Achieved the same thing borrowing someone's dog to look like we were just out for our evening walk. Nobody wants to stop a random guy who's just out walking a dog, especially if he might be holding a poop bag."

I laughed softly because it was certainly true. We just sat back and enjoyed our drinks for a while before either of us spoke again. It had been a much wilder night than we ever expected.

CHAPTER 16

I was dying. At least I felt sure I was dying. An acidic aftertaste of bourbon and cigarette smoke punctuated the sense that I probably should have been dying. That queasy feeling caused me to lift my head off the pillow and slowly take in the hatefully bright sunlight filtering in through the southern windows at the front of my house. Squinting down to survey the wreckage, I could see my future corpse was lying on the old red leather sofa in the front sitting room. In the overstuffed chair in one corner, a rumpled old timer was snoring. He was a familiar-looking big guy, with salt-and-pepper hair. My eyes slowly focused on him and I realized Archer was definitely looking pretty rough.

Heidi bustled into the room carrying two large mugs of coffee, startling Archer awake. "Good morning! The sun is up, there's birds singing somewhere, and you two look like death warmed over. Here's some liquid motivation," she said in her most chipper voice as she handed the mugs to us. "You're going to want to watch the news today," she added, ignoring the pained groans of thanks, or maybe acknowledgements, grunted by the living dead occupying the sitting room.

"Oh man, did anybody get the number of that train that hit us last night?" rumbled Archer after he got the first sip of coffee in him.

Heidi laughed aloud. "You two were so drunk when Annabelle brought you back, it was a miracle that we got you into the house. And those songs you guys kept singing! Like a couple of sailors on shore leave."

"Last night got pretty vague. When was closing time? 2 a.m.?" Archer asked. "Something like that. I really don't remember even leaving that dive bar we were holed up in."

Snorting, Heidi replied, "I'm not surprised. Neither of you boys were feeling any pain."

"Unlike now," I admitted. I was still squinting in the bright sunlight when my burner phone rang. It was Joel.

"Dad, I'm about a half-hour from your place. You ready?"

The hangover thickness between my ears was palpable, like a living creature scratching and clawing the dying brain matter up there. Needless to say, I was feeling a little slow and off my game because of it. "For?" I asked, drawing out the word.

"Thumb drive. It's time to get cracking," Joel said.

"What's up?" Archer asked, an eyebrow arched quizzically.

"Youth. It's totally wasted on the young. Joel's bringing the thumb drive over. I guess we'll try to figure out the encryption on the data," I grumbled. After last night, my gravelly voice sounded more like rock crushers than normal, so Archer just chuffed a small laugh over how I sounded.

By the time Joel arrived, we had gotten cleaned up and were looking like we might rejoin the living, assuming either of us was allowed near more polite company. Joel went straight into the office, and fired up the PCs in there. Thanks to some earlier adventures and investigations, we now had access to some pretty sophisticated spoofing and hacking tools that both Joel and Jeffrey were pretty talented at using. Archer and I thought some of those tools were probably illegal, but neither of us was inclined to look into that too closely.

"How long's this gonna take?" Archer asked, setting a fresh cup of coffee on the end table and settling back into the same chair he had slept in.

My shrug was interrupted by Joel's shout from down the hall. "I'm thinking about now sounds right," I replied. We both stood and walked to the office, coffees in hand.

"I got it," Joel announced upon our entry to the room.

"That was quick," Archer noted. "Now what do we do with all of the data?"

"It's time to do your homework, that's what you do with the data," Joel said. He pulled a thumb drive from the PC and inserted another one to make more unencrypted copies so we could all have a set to search from. "Their cipher was pretty weak."

I smiled and nodded. "That tracks with leaving the manufacturer's backdoor access in place on their system back at the union hall. Poor data management practices."

"Union hall? Was that you guys in Woodbury last night?" Heidi's horrified voice from behind froze the three of us in place like deer in headlights. Her demeanor meant I was about to beg for an easy death.

"You put our son in danger? And yourselves, too?" Heidi's voice turned dangerously frosty, and she stormed out of the room.

Joel chuckled. "Ooooh. You're a dead man, Dad. And she doesn't even know Jeffrey was there too."

Trading glances with Archer, he deadpanned, "I can just shoot you now. Just put you out of your misery."

I rolled my eyes. "You shoot like Helen Keller. I don't want to limp away from this wreck."

Archer guffawed. "Let's get to work." He took the drive Joel handed to him and opened a laptop PC.

I turned on the small TV in the office for us to listen to, and followed suit with the last available laptop in the room. Several minutes passed and the three of us had paid no attention whatsoever to our PC screens. We only had eyes for the TV because the local news was all over what they had already dubbed the Gunfight at the OK Corral. They were endlessly speculating about the ashy remains of one, possibly two, bodies that had been found inside the burned skeleton of a vehicle.

Archer chuffed. "Please tell me you had those spoofing apps running on our PCs last night."

I laughed. "Yep. They show all of us online shopping last night. You even put some stylish table lamps in your shopping cart while you slept on it."

"That's because I have good taste," said Archer dryly.

Once Northstar NewsHub began repeating its coverage of last night's fracas, our attention quickly focused on sifting through the stolen data. There was a lot of it.

* * *

"Breakthrough or nah?" Archer asked, taking a sip of his coffee. It was early morning on the third day of our research, and the house was quiet except for the two of us sifting through data.

"It's a solid schmaybe," I quipped. Archer rolled his eyes. I annoyed him when I used made-up words that could mean anything. He liked his language precise.

"So, what are we looking at?" Archer asked. It was a fair question because neither of us had a solid grasp of all this financial information.

Pointing with my chin towards the screen, I said, "I think we're looking at a state-level version of the USAID federal funding scandal. I think."

Eyebrows arching in surprise, Archer looked at me incredulously. "No shit?"

"No shit. If we're reading this right, the legislature heavily funded a fake charity run by Local 28240-A to the tune of about $250 million. Some of that funding went to legitimate causes like feeding the hungry, but that was merely window dressing to mask the graft that was disbursed to the real recipients. The union kept the lion's share, which it used to fund its short selling of Harrison's company stock. It looks like there's also dozens of officials on the dole, too. Judges, prosecutors, investigators, auditors and the like. The legislators who pushed the appropriations bill through to fund this charity also received hefty kickbacks."

"They must've thought their campaigns and retirement accounts were worthy recipients." Archer never took his eyes off the screen as he took in the document we had assembled from dozens of documents. The interconnection mapping I made looked like a small spider web. "What do we do with this?"

That was the million-dollar question. We had stolen data that revealed a huge financial scandal. Careers would end and crooks should go to jail. Putting away corrupt officials was all well and good, but it still doesn't completely solve the crime we were hired to solve. Loose ends needed to be tied together first. The first knot to tie was to send a copy of the stolen files to my Mysterious Friend.

* * *

"The Petition for Disinterment for Mr. Johnson is filed," announced Tavington. We were sitting in his office, and he had his feet up on his desk.

"When's the hearing date?" asked Annabelle.

"Next week. We're on an accelerated hearing basis because Judge Emhoff is clearing his calendar later. He's going on vacation somewhere," Tavington stated.

"That works for us," Archer said. "What do we do if Emhoff gives the next of kin the thumbs down?"

Annabelle answered. "He won't. He'll try to find a way to, but his hands will be tied." Her cryptic words caused the four of us to go quiet as we contemplated the import of Annabelle's statement.

Tavington hadn't been read in on what we found at the Union Hall, so he didn't know exactly what Annabelle meant. "We better be damn sure about that," Tavington said. Despite his relaxed posture, his face betrayed worry. "Cause if we drop the ball about this, he's gonna make us pay dearly."

CHAPTER 17

"Everyone please rise! The District Court of the Fourth Judicial District, County of Hennepin, State of Minnesota is now open. Judge Barry Emhoff presiding," announced the bailiff loudly. The attorneys and media in attendance stood for Judge Emhoff while he walked to the bench at the front of his courtroom. Because Judge Emhoff had accelerated his hearing calendar, the courtroom was filled with petitioners of all sorts seeking redress for various issues.

Soon, Tavington and Donna Johnson were seated at the petitioner's table. Tavington awaited Emhoff's signal to proceed, but instead Emhoff kept them waiting while he reviewed the Petition for Disinterment. Finally, Emhoff looked up at Tavington.

"Mr. Tavington, the Court has reviewed the Petition and does not find compelling reasons for the next of kin to disinter Mr. Johnson's remains from their current resting place," Emhoff stated without preamble.

Stunned, Tavington tried to speak but Emhoff shut him down. "Mr. Tavington, that is this Court's final ruling and the Court will not entertain further discussion about this Petition," Emhoff said flatly.

"Your Honor, there hasn't been any discussion at all. We'd like to make our record …" Tavington quickly said when Emhoff interrupted him again.

"Bailiff, escort Mr. Tavington and Mrs. Johnson from the courtroom. Mr. Tavington, another outburst like that and you'll be held in contempt of court."

A voice shouted from the gallery, "What about Local 28240-A? Your name is on their so-called charity list!"

Annabelle traded looks with Archer and me. It was a comical moment because we were all wearing similar eyeglasses. We didn't need to look and see who the speaker was, because we knew her voice, but we did so anyway. It was Northstar NewsHub's own Janey Petersen.

Petersen was standing tall amid the hubbub of the gallery and she held a notebook and pen in her hands.

Emhoff gaveled his displeasure and shouted "Order! Order in this Court!" His attempt at quieting down the courtroom only added fuel to the fire and created an uproar.

"What are you trying to hide, Judge?" Petersen shouted, more to be heard above the crowd than for dramatic effect. "Do you think Johnson's corpse holds the secret to unraveling more government fraud?"

Judge Emhoff angrily pointed his gavel right at Petersen and roared, "Bailiff! Arrest that woman!"

And the Bailiff did just that. She wasn't a physically imposing Bailiff, but she nonetheless pushed her way into the gallery and roughly grabbed Peterson and put her into an arm lock despite Peterson offering no resistance.

The expression on Peterson's face clearly said she had not expected to actually be manhandled by a Bailiff today, but she knew better than to put up a fight. Especially because she also knew she was being videoed despite Judge Emhoff's ban on cameras in his courtroom.

During the commotion, Tavington quietly walked Mrs. Johnson out of the courtroom. He hadn't thought highly of today's Plan B for the legal proceedings in case Emhoff wasn't amenable to the Petition, but he had still agreed to go along with triggering a kerfuffle by voicing his objection to Emhoff's brush off of the Petition. While Tavington wasn't willing to go to jail for the scheme, he had no problem with being the catalyst that would eventually expose corruption.

We had worked it out with Petersen in advance that she would interject her questioning from the gallery if things went south and Tavington had to try to make his record. None of us had expected Emhoff to react so poorly, but the abbreviated court appearance would make for dramatic TV viewing.

Peterson had agreed to go along with Plan B because she was counting on a scoop and the hoped-for protection of being a well-known media personality, but she had a few conditions. The primary condition was that the episode be captured on video and that NorthStar NewsHub immediately be given copies. Given our working history with Petersen and NorthStar NewsHub, we readily agreed. Accordingly, we arrived for court wearing smart glasses which recorded video of what we saw. Since we sat near Petersen, our video of her arrest was going to be excellent.

As the bailiff hustled a handcuffed Peterson from the courtroom, Emhoff shouted the court will recess for 30 minutes. We decided we needed to be elsewhere, so the three of us filed out along with numerous other folks who had been in the gallery. In minutes we were driving away in my black pickup truck and Annabelle uploaded the videos to NorthStar NewsHub while I drove.

Annabelle's phone rang, and she answered it on speakerphone. "Hello?"

"What in the hell happened?" roared Frank Testering, chief editor of NorthStar NewsHub.

"You watched the video?" Annabelle asked.

"Yes. The first video. Are they all the same?"

"Pretty much. The others were just taken from slightly different angles. Janey got hauled off and thrown into the slammer by Judge Emhoff," Annabelle said.

"I can see that! Why did she disrupt the proceeding?" Testering said. He was calming down a bit now. "What angle are you guys working here?"

"We're working a joint investigation with Janey. Did you catch the name she shouted out?"

"Uh. Some union. That wasn't what I focused on when I watched the video."

"Frank, that union is the key. The Local 28240-A union hall in Woodbury was where the Gunfight at the OK Corral took place last week," Annabelle added.

The stunned silence from Testering spoke volumes. I could picture the gears turning in his head over the unexpected connection to such a big local news story.

"Same union?" Testering finally asked, as if needing additional confirmation.

"Same outfit. Janey left you a copy of the union's data and her analysis of it on her shared drive, plus some instructions for how she wanted the report to broadcast," Annabelle said. "Janey—" Annabelle was saying when Testering interrupted.

"How do you know it's the union's data files and not something else?"

Annabelle smiled gently. "First off, I had nothing to do with it. The Gunfight at the OK Corral wasn't some gang war that got out of hand like you've been told by the authorities. We think it was a data heist that got interrupted by a couple of goons from the union."

"You *think*? What do you know?" Testering grumbled threateningly.

"Based on the data analysis connecting the dots linking state financing to the union's investments to payments to specific persons and NGO entities, yes, we do so think because we know the data was stolen that night and that appears to be the only thing that was taken by intruders. So does Janey." Annabelle didn't need to spell out to Frank that "NGO" meant Non-Governmental Organization.

"And you just … *happened* to find yourself in possession of this data." It was a statement, not a question and Testering's voice suddenly sounded suspicious. I could just imagine him slightly squinting at the mental picture he had of Annabelle.

"We received it through our anonymous 'Murder in Minnesota' sub-mission portal along," Annabelle stated quietly.

That was true enough. We had decided to create a new evidentiary data trail explaining how we came into possession of the data, so Jeffrey used a temporary email and a top-rated VPN to make the source of the upload virtually untraceable. Annabelle thought it was a nice touch that Jeffrey had sent the email using the WiFi at a busy coffee shop, which we knew lacked surveillance cameras. Afterwards, he brought the laptop over to Joel's house, whereupon they physically demolished it and scattered the leftover bits at the local dump. After that, we recreated the original hacking so a forensic search of our computers would only show we accessed the files after they were uploaded to the portal. Any evidence that we had actually accessed the files the morning after the theft and firefight had been carefully purged. It was just one more factor we could use to argue should some prosecutor decide to bring charges alleging that we had been involved in the fracas, which we had in fact totally been behind.

"The same 'Murder in Minnesota' submission portal that you so famously used to hamstring the State's false prosecution of you for the Zoe Finch murder?" Despite Testering's cynicism, he couldn't help but be slightly envious. The secrets this submission portal helped us expose during Annabelle's trial for Zoe's murder had gained significant street credibility among the media community. After that trial, podcast refer ences to more secrets uploaded to our submission portal became pretty constant. Most of those uploaded secrets came from followers of the show, many of whom are whistleblowers, but we were not above using it to create evidentiary trails for CYA purposes.

Annabelle sensed that Testering wasn't quite sold, so she forged ahead. "Our show will be reporting about the connection between a union front for laundering government money and three, possibly four, murders, and Martin Triton's wrongful conviction. Janey was going to focus on the money laundering scandal and efforts by corrupt government officials to keep it quiet. There's a lot to unpack, a lot of evidence to support the reporting. That means we have plenty of material for both of our outlets to report."

Testering finally made a decision and said, "OK. We need to do something about Janey, first."

Annabelle had broken Testering's will by dangling the prospect of exclusive scoops over a huge, government money laundering scandal. Northstar NewsHub needed ratings and clicks to survive in today's world, and partnering with "Murder in Minnesota" had been fruitful in the not-too-distant past. Northstar NewsHub had recently missed a scoop when they failed to report a story about the State having blown a $17 billion budget surplus on pet projects and extremist causes that benefited practically no one. Now the station needed to play catch-up on the government's sheer fiscal irresponsibility. Testering could not imagine a better way to take the lead than a huge scoop about this latest imbroglio.

Annabelle was already waiting with a suggestion about Petersen's fate. "Judge Emhoff throwing Janey in jail makes her a martyr. Once your outlet reports there are documents including Emhoff's name on them ..." she said, her voice trailing off. A phone's ringtone could be heard in the background.

"Hold on for a moment," said Testering gruffly, "while I take this call."

Archer, Annabelle and I all exchanged quick looks with each other while we waited. Testering quickly rejoined our call.

"That was Jonas, our legal counsel. He thought he was taking the day off. He thought wrong. What's your timeline for airing all this dirty laundry?"

Annabelle half-smiled. "We'd like to begin our initial shows tomorrow or the day after because Janey doesn't need to be sitting in a cell."

"Agreed. Let's shoot for tomorrow. I'd like to get a Petition filed for her release by then, and Jonas is going to need a little time to work one of those up. I'll call in our anchor to get her up to speed on what's happening. Are you up for working with her to coordinate the reporting? If we can get this on air for tomorrow's 6 o'clock news, that timing could work pretty well for us and as a lead-in to your podcast."

Annabelle looked at me and Archer for confirmation, and we both nodded to her so she told Testering we can do that. After the call ended, I spoke first.

"We need to bring Tavington up to speed so he's ready with an emergency appeal of the Petition for Disinterment that he can file after the initial reporting airs," I said. "Maybe it'll have more traction then."

Archer chuckled. "Maybe we'll finally be able to finish solving other mysteries so we can wrap up the original one that we signed up for?"

That caused a ripple of laughs from all three of us. It was going to be a tense couple of days.

CHAPTER 18

NORTHSTAR NEWSHUB BROADCAST – MINNEAPOLIS

Good evening, I'm Haley Blunt. Here at Northstar News-Hub, we have closely followed the recent violence that took place at the Local 28240-A union hall in an office park in Woodbury. The incident left two unidentified men dead, but could there be more to the story?

Yesterday, our own Janey Petersen was thrown in jail by Judge Barry Emhoff during a hearing. The family of Erik Johnson, a former employee of billionaire Martin Triton, was seeking court permission to exhume Johnson's body, which had been found in Lake Minnetonka. As you may recall, Mr. Triton was convicted of murdering his business rival, Bill Harrison, and he is serving a life sentence without possibility of parole.

After Judge Emhoff denied the Petition for Disinterment for Mr. Johnson, Northstar NewsHub reporter Janey Petersen shouted a question at Judge Emhoff. The video from that hearing was broadcast earlier today by the popular and influential "Murder in Minnesota" podcast team of private investigators. The video, exclusively made available to Northstar NewsHub, shows Judge Barry Emhoff order-ing Donna Johnson, the mother of Erik Johnson, and her attorney, Jerry Tavington, escorted from the courtroom by the bailiff. Attorney Tavington successfully defended Anna-belle Finch during her trial for the Bimbo Bits slaying of Zoe Finch last year. As they were leaving the courtroom, North-star NewsHub's Janey Petersen then asked this question:

[Janey Peterson] What about the Local 28240-A? Your name is on their so-called charity list!"

[Judge Emhoff] (banging of gavel) Order! Order in this Court!

[Janey] What are you trying to hide, Judge? Do you think Johnson's corpse holds the secret to unraveling more gov-ernment fraud?

[Judge Emhoff] Bailiff! Arrest that woman!

(Emhoff's bailiff pushed her way into the gallery and roughly grabbed Peterson, putting her into an arm lock despite Peter-son offering no resistance.)

Northstar NewsHub apologizes for that disturbing video, but we feel it sets the stage for what happened this afternoon. This morning, "Murder in Minnesota" released its latest episode on its investigation of the conviction of Martin Triton.

In that episode, and with links to documents uploaded to its submission portal that were purportedly obtained from the violent data heist at the Local 28240-A, "Murder in Minnesota" has questioned whether there is a connec-tion between alleged money laundering by the union, and the deaths of Erik Johnson, Bill Harrison, and the unex-

plained deaths of Martin Triton's wife, Samantha Triton and their neighbor, Tammy Kettle. The deaths of Mrs. Triton and Mrs. Kettle are under an active investigation as are the deaths of the two unidentified men whose vehicle was destroyed by a rocket propelled grenade in Woodbury.

Based on the union's documents that purport to identify Judge Barry Emhoff as a recipient of laundered government slush funds from Local 28240-A, our attorney has filed an emergency petition for the release of Janey Petersen from jail. We here at Northstar NewsHub will follow this story closely and report all developments as we receive them.

I tapped the power button on the remote to shut off the television. Everyone in Annabelle's living room started speaking at once. It was quite a scene. Heidi, all three of our children, plus spouses and our granddaughters were crowded into the space. Tavington and Archer were also there, so there wasn't a seat to spare. Drinks and hors d'oeuvres filled hands and plates. My little granddaughters even stopped playing long enough to look confused over the sudden explosion of talking before they went back to playing with the toys strewn about the sun room.

Tavington eventually tamped down the uproar enough for him to take the floor and say something. "OK, um. NN's report was a lot stronger than I expected. Based on how they phrased their reporting, NN is still making 'Murder in Minnesota' shoulder the defamation burden that the evidence is true," Tavington said, using NN as shorthand for Northstar NewsHub. "I don't wanna end up losing my license because we falsely accused the powers that be like some lawyer in the Dakotas did years ago."

I chuffed slightly. "We're old and crusty, and unlike that guy, we understand the strength of the evidence and what to do with it. Plus, we actually have the bank records and wire transfer records to prove it, which that guy lacked entirely. Most importantly, don't forget you aren't accusing anybody of anything, remember? You're just a lawyer trying to exhume a body on behalf of his grieving mother. We were damn careful to simply 'question' the propriety of actions taken given the contents of documents that we received and feel an investigation should get underway to substantiate the truth."

Tavington didn't look totally mollified, so Archer hammered home the point. "Look, Jerry. I don't have firsthand knowledge of all the legal procedural rules, but don't you think this at least lets you argue to the appellate court for a change of judge? If nothing else, our courts might want to avoid the appearance of any conflicts of interest."

"Especially if there is a heightened media interest in the case," Tavington nodded, thinking aloud but also unintentionally finishing Archer's thought. "We'll run with it. I'll file an emergency appeal and see if we can get this on the calendar."

Annabelle's cell phone buzzed. She looked at it and said, "It's one of the networks."

Before anyone else had a chance to say anything, my cell phone and Archer's buzzed simultaneously. Glancing at my phone screen, I noted, "Word's gotten out. I've got Northstar's parent network on my line."

"Attorney General's office on mine," Archer said. "Time to get back to work."

The rest of our evening was spent responding to phone calls and messages from national media, so Tavington went back to his office to prepare the emergency appeal. While we were occupied, Heidi, Riley and Auntie Natalie got our granddaughters off to bed when it was time for them to go to sleep. "Murder in Minnesota" had once again caused a local scandal to go viral with its investigations and reporting.

* * *

"What?" yelled Tavington. "OK, OK. I'll tell our client. Thanks, I think." It was late afternoon and he was sitting alone in his office. Shaking his head slightly, he dialed another number that was quickly answered.

"We need Old Fashioneds," Tavington said into his phone without preamble or banter. "My office. How soon can you get here?" He asked, listening intently. Nodding to himself, he said, "They'll be ready. See you boys in 10 minutes."

Hanging up the phone for a second time, Tavington stood and walked to the bar that was situated along one side of his office. Reaching into the mini-fridge, he removed an orange and his specialty ice cube tray, the kind that makes large, square ice cubes. Tavington had mastered the art of making ice cubes that are perfectly clear, and he deposited one cube apiece into three highball glasses sitting on his bar's countertop.

When Archer and I pushed through his office door, Tavington simply held out two glasses to us.

"How bad?" Archer asked before taking a sip of the Old Fashioned and grunting slightly in approval. By now, Archer had become part of our Old-Fashioned club and he recognized that we used it as our comfort drink. Something was wrong, and we were about to find out what it was.

Pursing his lips after taking a sip himself, Tavington looked at us for a long moment before speaking. "The Court of Appeals shot down our emergency appeal for Donna Johnson. They won't permit Erik Johnson's body to be exhumed."

"Well, shit," I exclaimed softly. "That makes it more difficult for Martin to win a Get Outta Jail Free card." I shook my head slightly as the three of us stood in a small circle near the bar.

"Difficult, but not impossible. We've been preparing the paperwork under the expectation that we wouldn't have that final piece of the puzzle to rely upon. Preparing for the worst," Tavington said with a rueful shrug. "I really, really wanted that evidence, though."

I took a big hit of the Old Fashioned and thought for a few moments while the other two aimlessly swirled the liquor in their glasses and looked glum. "Maybe it's better to beg forgiveness than to seek permission?" I suddenly said.

"What, are you going to snap your fingers and just resurrect the guy? The ground's getting harder and cemeteries don't let anyone just come in and start digging holes." Tavington couldn't help himself and his voice betrayed a hint of bitterness at the intransigence of the Court of Appeals despite a week of intense media scrutiny over the growing money laundering scandal.

Archer looked at me and raised his eyebrows in a non-verbalized question. A half-smile crept across my face as both of us looked at Tavington and said "We know a guy," in unison.

A pained expression ghosted across Tavington's face and he scoffed and shook his head slightly. "Why did I know you guys were going to say that?"

CHAPTER 19

The harsh glare magnified the shadows cast by the headstones, memorials and leafless tree branches in the cemetery. Wisps of cloudy vapors exhaled by the men were stolen away by a slight, nighttime breeze that made it feel much colder as the work commenced inside the cordoned-off worksite. Three men stood nearby as a backhoe bit into the grassy soil, their faces shadowed from the worksite lights behind them. The site was bracketed by orange and white striped Type I and II sawhorse barricades that were interconnected by long runs of bright yellow tape with the word "Caution" clearly visible. Blinking yellow lights affixed to the top of each sawhorse enhanced the legitimate look of the proceedings.

"This is bad business," muttered Tony Sorvino with a decidedly unenthusiastic expression on his face. He wore a hardhat and safety vest and stood with his hands thrust deep in his pockets. Sorvino never took his eyes off the growing hole being dug by his right-hand-man, Bruno, who was operating the backhoe. Bruno had little difficulty digging into the ground as it wasn't frozen rock solid this early in the season.

Archer and I exchanged glances at Sorvino's reticence. "I didn't think you'd get the heebie-jeebies over digging up a corpse," Archer said in a modestly surprised voice. Archer's face was slightly side-lit by blinking yellow light from one of the sawhorses.

"I have no problem making the bodies, but after that," Sorvino said, his head shaking slightly while he searched for the right words. "Messing with corpses is bad ju-ju."

I chuffed slightly, too softly for either man to notice. When I thought of Sorvino, him being squeamish around corpses would have been at the bottom of my list of adjectives to describe the man. That was as surprising to me as it was to Archer. Even more surprising was watching Bruno operate a backhoe with the degree of skill that he was displaying. I swear Bruno was having a good time at the controls of the machine that he clearly had mastered.

Almost as if summoned by Sorvino's words, the headlights of an SUV turning into the cemetery's distant front gates caught our attention. It wasn't 10 p.m. yet, so the gates were still open. As it drew closer, we could see that the SUV was a squad from the Chaska Police Department. The vehicle stopped, and a uniformed patrolman stepped out of the vehicle to approach us with a flashlight in his right hand. Sergeant stripes on his sleeves told us the man was no rookie.

"Evening, Officer. What's the good word?" Sorvino asked in his friendliest voice.

Glancing at the deepening hole, the officer lifted the flashlight to illuminate the three of us. "A bit late to be working, don't you …" he began saying when he suddenly interrupted himself. "Archer! What the hell are you doing here?"

"Terry, you old bastard! You still owe me $20," Archer exclaimed in surprise as he shook hands with the officer. "Why are you riding a squad at night? Don't have younger blood to go out and do the real work? You're a sergeant for chrissakes."

"Half of my uniforms are down with the Goo Flu, so both sergeants are out riding circuit tonight. And you don't get to collect on rigged bets, Archer. You knew she was a guy all along," the officer quipped.

Archer chuckled, then made introductions. "Sergeant Terry Brookings, meet my associates, Tony Sorvino and Dante Finch. Terry and I went to the academy together."

Brookings shook hands with each of us. "Gentlemen, any friend of Archer's," he said with a nod towards Archer, "is automatically a suspect."

I barked a laugh while Brookings and Archer chuckled at their old joke. "It's a pleasure. And truer words have never been spoken," I said with a conspiratorial nod towards Archer.

With a point of his chin towards the hole, Brookings said, "I suppose I don't wanna know what's going on here." He said it both as a statement and as a question.

"Correct in one," Archer replied. He didn't offer anything further.

"And if I would ask, you gents would have some sort of work order to show me, right?" Brookings continued in a leading tone.

"Also correct." Archer couldn't stop a half-smile from forming. "But we were never here," he added.

Brookings snorted a small laugh. "Well, far be it from me to get in the way of the working man. This related to that whole fracas with the Gunfight at the OK Corral and the union's money laundering scandal?" he asked. By now, our near-disaster at the union hall in Woodbury was commonly being called the Gunfight at the OK Corral around the metro.

Archer nodded as he watched the backhoe work before glancing back at Brookings. "Tangentially, at best. This is more to connect some of that stolen data that we later received to our investigation into the conviction of Martin Triton."

"The billionaire? I thought you guys were done with that investigation?" Brookings asked, startled. One effect of the Gunfight at the OK Corral was that it had nearly erased any coverage of Triton's investigation and attempts to win his release.

While I knew Brookings wasn't the union's payee because I had basically memorized the list, I wasn't sold on whether he would try to run us in. His earlier words hadn't totally convinced me, although Archer seemed at ease. Brookings next words sealed the deal, though.

"I hope you boys find what you're looking for. Disinfect them all with sunshine and broadcast it," Brookings said. "Give me something interesting to listen to for the next episodes." Whatever Brookings was going to say next was interrupted by an incoming call from Dispatch. After answering it, Brookings sighed tiredly and said, "No rest for the wicked."

"You, or your customers?" Archer quipped.

"Yes," said Brookings, answering vaguely since both were probably true. Brookings then turned and walked back towards the squad car. "Call me for the next poker night, Archer," he said loudly over his shoulder.

"I'll take your $20 from you then, Terry!" Archer called back.

Without looking back, Brookings acknowledged Archer's dig with a casual wave before he got into the squad and drove off to wherever he had just been sent to.

The three of us again faced the still-growing hole after Brookings drove off, and I traded confused glances with Sorvino for a moment. Then we both looked at Archer.

"Don't say it," Archer warned without taking his eyes from the hole. He knew peer pressure when he saw it.

Totally ignoring him, I asked, "You knew she was a guy all along?" The disbelieving tone of my voice clearly told Archer he wasn't going to get out of telling us what sounded like an interestingly sordid tale. "You wanna add to that for us?"

"Long story," was all Archer offered. Both Sorvino and I began chuckling at Archer's evasive non-answer.

It was Sorvino who said what I was thinking. Shrugging noncommittally and pointing towards the hole with a tilt of his head, Sorvino said, "We have all night."

Sighing, Archer rolled his eyes in exasperation. "I hate you guys." Then he proceeded to entertain us with a long story about a transvestite escort that he and Brookings once arrested and the bet they made.

* * *

"What do you mean you're dropping the Petition for Disinterment? I thought you wanted to connect the death of Johnson to Harrison as part of the effort to get Martin Triton out of jail? Did I miss something?" Frank Testering's rapid-fire questions conveyed his irritation that Northstar NewsHub may have been left out of something important in the media furor over the growing money laundering scandal of Local 28240-A. "Did Jesus roll the rock back on Johnson's tomb or something so we can't exhume the body?"

Annabelle, Archer, Tavington, Janey Petersen, and myself were seated in Frank Testering's small office at Northstar NewsHub. With every available seat taken, it felt cramped and crowded, which couldn't have improved Testering's mood.

"Something like that. Frank, we were kept in the loop. NN is receiving copies of the toxicology and genetic testing reports at the same time as Annabelle's gang," Petersen said gently.

"Testing? On whom?" growled Testering. He was confused because he didn't know what had happened or how accurate his quip actually was. Yet.

"Of Mr. Johnson's corpse. He was exhumed without a court order, and those tests are being run to both confirm his identity and to ascertain whether he was poisoned," Annabelle answered before Petersen could. "We think this is the final piece of the puzzle."

Testering, for all his crusty exterior, couldn't have looked more surprised had Godzilla stormed into his office wearing a pink tutu and started tap dancing to show tunes. He looked at us for a few, long moments, before he tiredly rubbed his eyes. Then he asked, "How did you get a hold of his body? A grave robber or something?"

"We hear it may have been something like that. Somebody dug him up on behalf of his mother, and now the test results will be uploaded to both NN and our submission portal. After that, Jerry will move forward with filing motions for Mr. Triton's release based on whatever those test results show," I summarized with a nod towards Tavington. "Either way, this is the likely conclusion of the particular mystery we were actually hired to investigate. From that point on, we'll continue to provide NN with whatever we can while NN continues reporting on the related money laundering scandal."

That seemed to satisfy Testering as he leaned back into his seat to digest what he had been told. Northstar NewsHub's ratings were back in the stratosphere thanks to the brouhaha arising from the Gunfight at the OK Corral, and he wanted those ratings to stay there. It was also now apparent to him that his station had not missed out on anything for which he wanted to be kept in the loop. He sighed, and said, "Alright. I guess I shouldn't be surprised dead bodies have inexplicably risen again when 'Murder in Minnesota' is in the mix. It's not like there's no precedent for a baffling, unexplained phenomenon around you guys after the Bimbo Bits killing in Prior Lake. OK. Janey, I want you to sketch out the broad strokes of how we'll report this when Tavington files the new motions. We'll need to be flexible depending on whether the toxicology provides a possible link between Johnson's cause of death and Harrison's."

"You got it, Chief," said Petersen.

"I suppose I have you guys to thank for making sure we have plausible deniability for the Johnson body being back above ground?" Testering asked gruffly.

Annabelle shrugged noncommittally. Her face wore the same "who me??" expression that I had occasionally seen when she was growing up. It was as insincere now as it was then. Right now we all wore versions of the same expression, even Petersen.

Testering rolled his eyes at the lot of us. "I'm surrounded by comedians. Don't quit your day jobs," he muttered. Then he ruefully smiled and said, "Alright, off with all of you. We've got work to do."

We bustled out of Testering's office and went our separate ways. No one said anything other than a quick goodbye to Petersen until after we were outside.

"How long until we see those reports?" Archer asked Tavington as we walked back to our cars.

Tavington shrugged. "Maybe ten days or so? Hard to say given the decomposition of Johnson's remains. I gotta go meet with Martin and make sure he and Terry Triton are sitting tight. We don't want them jumping the gun and asking Kristie Calwis for help again. Wrong skill set and all that."

"You going to represent Martin for the next motion?" I asked. It was a fair question since Calwis had essentially flamed out last time. Tavington was a proven player in the criminal law arena, while a family law expert like Calwis was the metaphorical square peg for a round hole.

Tavington nodded. "Terry already asked that question. They've flashed the cash and I don't believe there will be a conflict of interest. I'll tell them 'yes' today." He glanced at his watch, and looked up at us. "It'd be nice if the prep we did for the Petition for Disinterment could be carried over into Martin's motion, but that line of information is really just a horse of a different color that would be useless for Martin. So I've got to cobble a whole new motion and brief together from scratch."

"Work your magic, Jerry. You need anything, let me know. Assuming the test results show us something important, you good with coordinating the filing of the motion with the release of the test results?" I asked.

Tavington nodded. "Oh yeah. That would be helpful to make it public knowledge just after we file. It'll help keep Martin's appeal on the front burner. And speaking of urgency, I've got to get going. Terry and Martin are expecting me shortly."

Tavington soon sped away while Annabelle handled the driving for those of us returning to Prior Lake. The car ride home was pretty quiet as the three of us mulled over our team's investigation of Martin Triton's conviction. Everyone was thinking about whether we had missed something, how to continue presenting what we had uncovered for the show, and hoping there weren't going to be any unseen ramifications from our actions. State law enforcement had already contacted us to confirm how we had received the union's data through the submission portal, but as far as I knew there was no movement towards obtaining a search warrant to review our records and computer systems.

The lack of a search warrant pleasantly surprised me, to be blunt. Archer had thought it might be because whoever was in charge of law enforcement really didn't want to look too closely for reasons of their own. It could be because they might be afraid of what more they find, or it could be because the scandal had badly hurt all the right people. It really depended on which side that power was on. Either way, both Archer and I had further agreed they didn't find anything to pin the break-in and firefight on us because we would already be in jail if they had. At most, all they could prove was that we were home, shopping online, during the fracas, and that we had later received the stolen data anonymously through our submission portal. Archer had even ordered one of the lamps that went into his online cart that fateful night.

So now, all we had to do was wait for the latest events that were already in motion to develop.

CHAPTER 20

When Archer called the next morning, I learned events were developing rather quickly. I was also not expecting what he had to say.

"Dante, did you see the morning news?" he asked, sounding pretty concerned.

My ears perked up immediately. "Uh, no. I just stumbled out of the shower a few minutes ago. What's up?"

"Do you remember who Walter Ruggerein is?"

A dark sense of foreboding exploded in my gut as that name sparked the notion that I should recognize it. "My mental Rolodex is offline. Connect the dots for me."

"Ruggerein is, was, the president of Local 28240-A."

Archer's phrasing caught my attention. "Was? How "was" are we talking?" I asked.

"He was, until somebody bodied him last night and left his bimbo bits scattered around his place in Eagan. His housekeeper found what was left of him this morning." Archer delivered the news in his old, professional voice. One that conveyed all the scintillating excitement of reading a phone book aloud.

Shocked, I didn't know what to say for a few moments before a more practical question barged its way into my head. "Ruggerein being churned into bimbo bits didn't stop anyone from making a positive ID of the man?"

Archer grunted a small chuckle. "Fair question. I'm told his face was still intact. Northstar NewsHub is likewise reporting it was him."

"You're told? You got a contact on the scene?" I asked, confused.

"Yep. A couple of them. Guys I partnered with back in the day," Archer replied. "Nothing's faster than the WYK network."

I knew from working with him that Archer's quip about the WYK network referred to "who you know." We all have a WYK network, some networks being larger than others. "Was a motive for the killing announced? Are there suspects?" I asked quickly. I was pretty sure there would be a whole lot of nothing about motive and suspects. I was also dead wrong.

"Yeah. About that. The badges haven't released any information about motive or suspects, but my contacts privately told me a message was painted in the guy's blood on the wall of his living room. It said, "Pay your debts." That mean anything to you?" Archer asked wishfully. He was probably hoping I could solve this new mystery.

Thunderstruck, that phrase suddenly dredged up a frightening memory. Just in the past few weeks I had heard another cryptic reference to paying debts and the union. While my heart raced, I mentally replayed how I had sent the stolen union data to my Mysterious Friend, by way of an anonymous, temporary email address masked by a multi hop VPN that had been connected to a burner phone I purchased with cash. The chances of tracking it from my Mysterious Friend all the way back to us were as near to zero as possible. It would seem that anyone could have sent it.

That anonymity also raised another question in my head. I was surmising that my Mysterious Friend had someone end Ruggerein based on a WAG, which is my personal acronym for wild ass guess. The universe of bad actors who have grudges to settle with the union seemed to grow every day because of the data breach during the Gunfight at the OK Corral.

"So, anybody implicated in the money laundering scheme now has an axe to grind with the union for poor security, and a message was sent. That's what's going on? Dozens upon dozens of possible suspects?" I asked. While I would certainly wonder about whether my Mysterious Friend was implicated, the reality was that many could have done it.

Archer chuckled ruefully. "The list of possible suspects is long and illustrious. You hear from any investigators or find out anything new, give me a holler. We certainly don't want to get swept up into more of the union's tangled web of problems."

After hanging up, the phone rang as if the next caller was watching to see when my line was free. It was Annabelle's latest burner phone number. It wasn't hard to imagine what she's calling about.

"Dad! Did you see the news about the union president?" Annabelle said worriedly. From the background noise, I could tell she was driving somewhere.

"Not yet, but I just got off the phone with Archer about it. He has some contacts on the scene who gave him a heads up," I said. "Neither of us has any idea who did it," I added.

Annabelle chuckled softly. "Yeah, that's the understatement of the year. There's so many dirty players who the media already dragged into the light. Gotta be more than a couple of them who wanted to end Ruggerein and get some payback."

As with Archer, I didn't voice my suspicion there may be another dirty player who could have ruined Ruggerein's week. The lack of concrete connection to the crime is the same problem we encountered during the original Bimbo Bits investigation and false prosecution of Annabelle for the slaying of our distant relative. Unsubstantiated suspicions, but no real proof of who did it.

I'd love to cut ties with my Mysterious Friend. As far as I can tell, he's damn dangerous. Unfortunately, for the time being I'm metaphorically chained to the guy. I don't know his true identity, where he is, who works for him, or who his friends are. All I really know is he is careful and devious and has some devoted henchmen. How far his reach extends is a complete unknown outside of having learned my loyalty lesson from the prosecution for Zoe's death that we are definitely within his reach. It's a very disconcerting "relationship," for lack of a better description, but not entirely one-sided. Mysterious Friend also watches out for his people and that can be pretty important for loyalty.

"I'm heading over to meet Janey at the scene. Both her and Testering called and wanted us to drum up whatever we can. You want to meet us over there?" Annabelle asked.

Annabelle's question snapped me back to the present. Ruminations about Mysterious Friend weren't going to accomplish anything today. I wasn't going to call the guy and ask if he had someone carve up Ruggerein to send a message. I really didn't want to know the answer. Assuming Mysterious Friend would have admitted to anything, which he obviously would not.

"Nah, I'll sit this one out. I don't think me lurking around another crime scene is going to be all that productive," I replied. "You go ahead and call if you need something."

"Alright, Dad. If anything interesting comes up, I'll let you know." Annabelle cut the call and I went downstairs to make the morning coffee more out of habit than for some need for it. Those two calls were more than sufficient to wake up anybody.

Hours later, I received a text from Archer asking if we could meet at The Swamp. It was late afternoon when Annabelle and I arrived at Archer's place. We were soon gathered around his kitchen table, staring at his laptop PC.

"Where did you get this video, exactly?" Annabelle asked. She hadn't taken her eyes off the screen while asking.

"Wait 30 seconds, and then you'll get one guess." Archer offered nothing more while we watched.

Not sure what we were seeing, I simply watched. The indoor scene in the video was from a home security camera hidden up near a ceiling corner. It appeared to be in an opulent living room with a fire burning in a marble fireplace along one wall. The space was obviously richly decorated with expensive furniture and décor. For the first twenty seconds, the room was empty and then until two men entered. The older of the two men appeared to be in his 60s, and built like a brick garage. He looked like a man used to breaking lesser mortals in half using only his bare hands. I noted he had gray hair, a thick, gray mustache, and dark eyes that conveyed no warmth.

The gray-haired man was in an animated argument with the second guy. I was shocked to recognize him even though we had only briefly met once. He had swarthy skin, and the black hair peeking out from underneath a black stocking cap was going gray. Crow's-feet wrinkles at the corners of his black eyes, even on security cam footage, nonetheless seemed to convey that the man had seen some awful things during his time. These dead eyes were utterly humorless and were the window into the man's heart of darkness. It was Word Man. He was back.

From previous experience, all I know is the appearance of Word Man means some bad shit is about to go down. Neither Archer nor Annabelle was aware of who Word Man was, or that we've met. If there was ever a deep, dark secret I had to keep from my friends and family, Word Man and the Mysterious Friend were definitely it.

After a few more moments of argument between Word Man and Grey-Haired Man about repayment of debts, Grey-Haired Man suddenly shoved Word Man as the emphasis for whatever point Grey-Haired Man was making. It was the wrong thing to have done. As if by magic, a wicked-looking knife appeared in Word Man's hand and he stabbed the blade straight into Grey-Haired Man's stomach.

What happened next wasn't just gruesome; it was next level horrifying. Word Man carved Grey-Haired Man into bloody pieces, callously tossing the pieces aside. Before the grisly operation was completed, Archer stopped the nightmarish video replay.

"Holy shit! What did we just watch?" Annabelle yelled. She looked absolutely stunned. "Ruggerein's home security footage of some thug carving up Walter Ruggerein into hamburger patties, that's what." Archer quipped grimly. "And, no, we can't put that video up for general consumption. It'll blow the cover of my contacts who gave it to me."

I grunted my agreement. I was thinking we'd never want to post something like that anyway unless we absolutely had to. There were enough copycat killers in the world — none of them needed to see this sort of thing.

By now I figured Archer had brought us here to talk about protecting ourselves. "There's too much at stake from the data breach and some serious players are out there. We need to proceed with extreme caution. Stay armed at all times. As far as anybody knows, we only made data publicly available after it had been sent to us. Same as Northstar NewsHub. But that doesn't mean somebody out there doesn't think lessons can't be taught by making examples out of any of us," Archer cautioned.

Archer wasn't wrong, but I just couldn't tell him there was more to the slaying of Ruggerein than met the eye. Since Archer's cautionary wisdom was still good advice because the union's beehive had been kicked a couple times, I wasn't going to stop him from coaching us up with pointers for staying safe.

I did my best to appear to pay close attention to Archer's safety instructions, but my head was certainly elsewhere. Word Man's sudden appearance on secret security video at the Ruggerein residence was stunning enough. What he proceeded to do on said video went far beyond that. It deficd description and I was pretty sure I would never be able to unsee what I just saw. It was also the most definitive proof in the world that the stolen data possibly played a role in my Mysterious Friend settling a score he had with the union. Given how cheap life seemed to be to my Mysterious Friend, I had to imagine that the settlement was vastly worse than the debt ever was. This also served to make me even more fearful of the involuntary 'relationship' with my Mysterious Friend. One wrong move, or a simple refusal to do his bidding, and some henchman of his might grind you or your family into hamburger.

The next few days passed relatively quietly, unless you were a Northstar NewsHub reporter. The new outlet was positively jumping with the continuing fallout of the money laundering scandal that now had at least a dozen killings tied to it as the dead bodies kept falling. While they included the deaths we already knew about — Tammy Kettle and Samantha Triton, the guys at the union hall during the night of the gunfight, Ruggerein and the now reported connection to Erik Johnson and Bill Harrison — the death toll had subsequently risen to include several others who had received large payments from the union. People were being bodied to keep them quiet under the tried and true axiom that dead men tell no tales.

Sometimes, however, there were exceptions to the rule that the dead tell no tales. That exception applied to the corpse of Erik Johnson.

CHAPTER 21

November was steadily growing colder. Most trees in Prior Lake had lost their leaves except for a few varieties stubbornly holding on. The linden tree in my yard was a good example of the latter; its leaves were still green. But, except for the pines, the trees surrounding The Swamp were mostly bare and we could now see the other three homes lining the reedy pond that were normally hidden during summer.

Tavington, Annabelle, Archer and myself were sitting in Archer's sunroom while the electric fireplace in the corner kept us warm. Coffee mugs were steaming, with more perking in the coffee maker. We were deep into discussions on how to wrap up our work on the Martin Triton affair.

"Not gonna lie. It's going to feel good to finally push this investigation past the finish line," Annabelle said.

Her blue eyes weren't really focused on anything in particular as she unconsciously swirled around some sort of honey infused coffee concoction in Archer's prized "People Lie, Evidence Doesn't" mug. Annabelle loved coffee, but she rarely drank it straight. I'd seen her make many kinds of coffee, frappe, lattes — she'd dress them up with all sorts of mixes. The kid had always been a foodie and loved to try to make new things in the kitchen.

Archer was used to Annabelle's quirky coffee ways. Somewhat. By now, he loved her like a second father, and would only share his prized mug with her — Tavington and I were kept a safe distance away from it. I had no doubt, though, that it pained him to see Annabelle's vile coffee concoctions swirling around in that mug. As for Archer, he was what could loosely be termed a "coffee enthusiast," which is a nice way of saying the man was nearly addicted to coffee. He took his straight up, black with no frou-frou stuff mixed in. Archer often joked that he liked his coffee like his women — dark, hot and very bitter.

"Any further inquiries from local law enforcement?" Tavington asked. Ever practical, he was always mindful of managing the team's risk exposure.

Everybody shook their heads. "Nah," Archer answered for the rest of us. "After their initial inquiries peaked, I think they lost interest in us because later events simply overwhelmed them."

Annabelle laughed. "Well, yeah. They have no evidence that we did anything wrong, but plenty of evidence that everyone else did a lot wrong. I think they're also a bit gun shy after we made everything public. Well, us and NN, and the feeding frenzy that followed, anyway."

I snorted a small laugh. "After the original Bimbo Bits debacle, they also have to realize they better be ready to protect their own asses if they come after us for exposing their mistakes. That history was set in stone after their fraudulent prosecution of Annabelle was dismissed," I said as everyone cracked small grins that contained very little humor.

Those had been frightening days. I had been afraid my daughter was going to be railroaded into being a prisoner for the killing of Zoe Finch. Annabelle had not committed that murder, of that I was certain. I was less certain of who might have, but I strongly suspected it was someone working for my Mysterious Friend and he was proving their point that I was now working for him. Because of that history, I thought it was better for our health if the killer's true identity remained unknown. As a practical matter, I also had no clear ideas that I could draw from to find that true identity, so that made for an unhappy alignment of harsh realities.

Tavington's cell phone rang, and he looked at the caller ID in surprise for a moment before answering. "It's the lab," he said.

If Tavington had wanted us to shut up and give him our full attention, there wasn't anything on Earth that he could have said more effectively than "It's the lab." We weren't expecting to hear from them until after Thanksgiving.

"Tavington. Yes. Uh huh. Really? How sure is sure? Oh, OK. Even I can do that math. You're sending the reports to me? Excellent. Thank you for the fast turnaround. Yeah, always nice to push the work through and clear up your table ahead of the holiday. Appreciate it."

"And?" Annabelle prompted. Her bright blue eyes were boring holes into Tavington with her intense anticipation.

Tavington sighed and reached for the carafe of coffee. He spoke as he poured. "That was the lab we hired to run tests on Mr. Johnson's remains. They detected the same trace elements of hemlock in his system as in Harrison. Both of them died by poisoning," Tavington summarized dramatically. He then took a deep sip of his coffee while the rest of us yelled versions of "I knew it!" It took a few minutes for us to settle down, and the realization that we still hadn't gotten over the finish line started to weigh heavily once again.

Sighing, I sat back while holding my cup of coffee with both hands and tried to wrap my head around the sprawling scope of what we had gotten mixed up in. The team had finally uncovered the stories behind the intertwined Triton-Johnson-Harrison-Kettle and Local 28240-A mystery. You could even include Anderson in that entanglement although he mostly followed his own agenda that, at times, had differed substantially from Martin's. This investigation had been much more difficult than any of our prior work, including when we were desperately trying to win Annabelle's freedom from the false prosecution for Zoe's murder.

We had employed surveillance, breaking-and-entering, bugged a home, came within spitting distance of blackmail, and theft. Then we triggered a spate of violence that was still cascading between participants in the illegal schemes we had exposed. Yet, despite all our questionable practices, I still didn't think we were the bad guys. Not really. Sometimes you simply did what you had to just to survive or succeed.

This time, we had succeeded. There had been a dangerous, secretive and well-financed cabal we had exposed while we investigated Harrison's murder. The irony wasn't lost on me that we probably wouldn't have looked too closely into them if they hadn't preemptively ended Samantha Triton and Tammy Kettle in a bid to silence them. Instead, it had the opposite effect. That miscalculation by the crooked kleptocrats and their "union" friends had unintentionally opened a window into their fraud and money laundering.

Conversation had stopped, and I was startled out of my reverie when I realized everyone was looking at me expectantly. "I'm sorry, I was in a happier place. Say again?" I said.

Archer chuffed and repeated his question. "You going to be ready for our next episode? The one where we truly wrap everything up and go on to the next investigation?"

I nodded slightly. "Yep. Good to go. Let's record it when Jerry receives the reports about Johnson and we look them over."

We didn't have long to wait. Those reports landed in Tavington's inbox within minutes and we eagerly pulled them up to read.

By mid-afternoon, we were ready for our next show.

"Murder in Minnesota," The Trifecta of Terror, finale episode excerpt:

> *[Annabelle] OK, everybody, it's time to quit teasing her identity and introduce one of today's special guests. Northstar NewsHub's esteemed, intrepid and doggedly determined reporter, Janey Petersen! Welcome back to the show, Janey. We're always excited to have you here at our Minnesota Mommy Studios. I know my daughter just adores you to pieces.*

[Janey] Oh, I'm just here for your daughter's hugs. You're the one who's making me work. Now I know what your dad's so-called retirement feels like.

(Annabelle's laughter mixed with the roars of laughs from Dante and Archer who are also in the studio.)

[Annabelle] You folks who are listening only and not watching the video can't see this, but my dad just dramatically motioned toward Janey with a "See! Janey feels my pain!" gesture while the rest of us got a chuckle out of the two of them. Janey, this episode is being released just before tonight's airing of NorthStar NewsHub's big exposé. That broadcast is going to be one you don't want to miss, folks. Trust us. Janey, Haley Blunt, and even Chief Editor Frank Testering, have been hard at work to expose one of the biggest scandals in Minnesota since, since, um …

[Archer] Since you were falsely prosecuted by a corrupt Attorney General's Office because Zoe Finch was chopped into Bimbo Bits?

(guffaws in the studio)

[Annabelle] Nah. This is bigger than that. This directly impacts far more people. Janey, you want to bring us up to speed on what NorthStar NewsHub has in store for tonight?

[Janey] Annabelle, you are certainly right about this being an important show tonight. While the Local 28240-A scandal came to light as a byproduct of the phenomenal investigative work by the "Murder in Minnesota" investigative team on behalf of jailed billionaire Martin Triton, for a reporter, this corruption scandal has become the gift that keeps on giving. We'll take our viewers behind the facade

of legitimacy projected by the union, and dispel the myths and fairy tales spun by government officials seeking to keep taxpayer money flowing into their pockets directly or through certain non-governmental organizations. We will be showing highlights of our forensic audit of government officials who pocketed public money and connecting some dots for our viewers.

[Annabelle] Wow. That is A LOT to digest, Janey. NorthStar NewsHub's show tonight is must-see TV. And the impacts are both widespread and personal for the NN news team, isn't that true?

[Janey] Indeed it is very personal for me, Annabelle. We will replay the courtroom video of my illegal arrest by order of Judge Emhoff, who we have identified as a significant recipient of state funds laundered through the union. He's the same judge that kept Mr. Triton in jail despite conclusive evidence of his innocence.

[Archer] Same judge? It was an even closer tie-in than just that. It was during the very same hearing that he denied the Petition for Disinterment of Mr. Johnson's corpse and had you keelhauled out of his courtroom. Seeing his name as a major recipient of funds certainly calls those actions into question.

(Annabelle makes a hand motion trying to get Archer to further explain the connection between Johnson and the Local 28240-A scandal.)

[Archer] We strongly suspected there was a connection between the union, Judge Emhoff, and Erik Johnson that motivated the judge to refuse to even entertain the Petition. Thanks to solid investigative reporting by both our

organizations, we've proven Mr. Johnson was poisoned by Samantha Triton and her lover Tammy Kettle using the same substance that killed Mr. Harrison, and that both their deaths were made to appear as if they were from other injuries. So, why is that important and how does this eventually connect to the union? That takes some background, which we will discuss right now.

Johnson was an employee of Triton Industries, but he was secretly being paid by Harrison in a case of industrial espionage. Then Martin made Johnson a better offer to become a double agent and used Johnson to feed Harrison false information in a scheme to bring down Harrison's company. Johnson visited Harrison's home the night of Harrison's death and his remains were later found floating in Lake Minnetonka several months after Harrison's demise.

[Dante] For Martin's plan to work, both Johnson and Harrison had to be alive. Both Martin and Harrison wanted to snap up their rivals' business at a deep discount. Martin's best route to do so was to use Johnson as a double agent to keep leading Harrison to make bad business decisions over a lengthy period of time that strengthened Martin's company at the expense of Harrison's.

There were two prongs Martin used to control Johnson. Firstly, Martin gave Johnson a financial stake in Triton Industries that would become significantly more valuable if they were successful against Harrison's company. Secondly, to seal the deal, Martin's wife, Samantha Triton, helped maintain control of Johnson through sex. And Johnson's stake was such that Martin needed him alive afterward because he would have some influence over Johnson's stake pursuant to their agreement. Losing Johnson meant losing his influence, which he needed to stay in control.

[Annabelle] What happened?

[Archer] After Samantha took control of the company by framing Martin for Harrison's murder, she needed to consolidate her power because her prenuptial agreement with Martin would strip her of control for infidelity. That meant she needed to eliminate evidence of her infidelity, which was the love triangle between Samantha, Tammy, and Ryan Anderson, Triton Industries' Security Chief. Samantha and Tammy plotted to kill Anderson, but the plot was foiled by law enforcement with the help of our "Murder in Minnesota" team.

[Annabelle] If it wasn't in Martin's interest to body Harrison and Johnson, why did Martin get convicted of their murder? That seems like a loose end.

[Dante] Well, the loose end was actually Martin himself. He discovered Samantha's additional infidelities after Tammy snapped up the discounted stock, and both Harrison and Johnson were dead. Martin confronted Samantha about it, and learned to his horror that Samantha was behind it all. Samantha was gaining control over the company and eliminating her competition when they became an inconvenience.

[Janey] But not nearly as inconvenient as getting arrested herself. This is where the ties to Local 28240-A began surfacing.

[Dante] Indeed. Samantha and Tammy ended up in jail for failing to take down Anderson, the security chief. They

thought to bide their time to avoid suspicion if he died too close in time to the first deaths, but the clock ran out when "Murder in Minnesota" came along and the game changed. But then something that should have been impossible happened. Both of them were murdered, not by Martin for their attempt to take over Triton Industries, but by the union. It was trying to hide its short selling of Harrison's company stock due to the acquisition of Dakota Aerospace by Triton Industries.

After Harrison's company, Dakota Aerospace, was acquired at a deep discount due to the espionage, Triton Industries replaced Dakota Aerospace stocks with new Triton Industries stock. That replacement basically erased records of the earlier short sale which had been funded by Local 28240-A. So, the union leaders figured since Martin was already sidelined by Samantha and Tammy, they could take both women off the board by having them killed and use their influence to suppress discovery of their money laundering through short selling. After all that happened, the cheaply acquired Triton Industries stock quickly increased in value when the acquired business was brought back into profitability by Triton Industries. Local 28240-A then began divesting of the stock at a huge profit and no one would have known.

[Annabelle] It might have worked, but what happened?

[Archer] Too much light was being shined on Tammy and Samantha by our investigation and the union had grown nervous from that. Then the Gunfight at the OK Corral went down, that's what happened, and the union offed them to keep them silent. While Samantha and Tammy's murders were being investigated, parties unknown broke into the Local 28240-A union hall and stole union data. By

now, we've heard so many theories on that particular who-dunit, it seems that everyone is pointing fingers at everybody else. What we do know is someone with an axe to grind with the Local 28240-A made sure both NorthStar NewsHub and "Murder in Minnesota" received copies of the union's stolen data because they would ensure the truth got out.

[Janey] Which brings us all to where we are today. A pair of convoluted schemes that collided at an inopportune time for all the players on each side. Cascading revelations of corruption, money laundering, theft, fraud, and a bloody trail of bodies. Lives and careers have been destroyed, and families torn apart. NorthStar NewsHub has a jam-packed, three-hour special exposé tonight. There is a lot to go over, and we move the reporting along at a fast clip. Don't miss it.

Soon after this episode went live, its downloaded numbers ranked up in the millions. The audience had supersized since before Samantha and Tammy died because it was already a sordid tale of espionage, sex and murders, with a jailed billionaire who had been framed for the worst of it. After the ladies died, quickly followed by the Gunfight at the OK Corral going down along with a bunch of bad actors, it became the biggest story anywhere. Despite everything that occurred, it wasn't until now that the last part of the Martin Triton investigation was ready to conclude.

CHAPTER 22

"Everyone please rise! The District Court of the Fourth Judicial District, County of Hennepin, State of Minnesota is now open. Judge Carrie Jackson presiding," announced the bailiff loudly. The attorneys and media in attendance stood for Judge Jackson while she walked to the bench at the front of her courtroom.

"Be seated. The Court has a full slate today, so we're going to get right to it."

Judge Jackson was in her late forties, and ascended to the bench after a decade serving as counsel, then as chief counsel, for the Republican caucus of the state legislature. She had built a solid reputation as a straight shooter and, in her time dealing the other side of the aisle of the legislative branch, had developed a rhino-like thick hide to deflect their racist slings and arrows. Many a white DFL (Democratic-Farmer-Labor) legislator had mistakenly suggested that they knew what was better for black attorneys like Jackson than she did. The Republican legislators merely sat back and watched her crush another condescending DFL representative like a bug. The Republicans had even organized a betting pool among themselves with odds on who among the other party would be foolish enough to cross swords with Jackson next.

As a judge, Jackson ran an efficient courtroom. Always looking for the truth, she had no patience for litigants and their attorneys who try to hide the truth behind a veneer of procedural rules. Jackson made no pretense that justice should ever be sacrificed upon the altar of convenience or comfort, and she zealously pushed to uncover truth in her courtroom.

"First on today's agenda is a Motion filed by attorney Jerry Tavington seeking to overturn the murder conviction of Martin Triton. Representing the State is prosecutor Ann Morris. Are both parties ready to proceed?" Judge Jackson asked.

"Defense is ready, your honor," Tavington announced from where he stood behind the defense table.

"Your Honor, the State asks for a continuance ..." Morris began saying when Judge Jackson interrupted.

"For what reason?"

"Unfair surprise, Your Honor. The State needs adequate time to prepare to meet the new defense allegations regarding the alleged circumstances of Mr. Harrison's death ..." Morris replied, but Judge Jackson interrupted her again.

"The media has talked about little else for weeks on end, Ms. Morris. And that information was also provided to you weeks ago. What do you propose to learn from a delay that hasn't already become common knowledge?"

Like nearly everyone else in Minnesota, Judge Jackson had been following our show and the incessant reporting of NorthStar NewsHub over the intertwined scandals. Even though she hadn't referenced why she had replaced Judge Emhoff for this matter, it was a small leap to conclude that everyone well knew why he had been completely removed from the bench instead of merely being reassigned from Triton's hearing. The union had paid Emhoff to shut down all inquiries into union funding no matter how remote, and that had included discovering the truth about Erik Johnson's death. Now Emhoff was out on bail and awaiting trial from the opposite side of the bench while all of his prior rulings in all cases were scrutinized or overturned.

Judge Jackson's question caught Morris by surprise. She tried to answer it as best she could. "Well, Your Honor, the, ah, toxicology testing hasn't been confirmed for starters. The State hasn't had enough time to review any of their alleged findings that are being offered to support their motion. The State asks for a delay of three months to be ready."

Looking over to Jerry, Judge Jackson merely asked, "Mr. Tavington, what's your position?" Jackson was careful not to telegraph her thoughts to either party.

Tavington was well prepared and he elected to use strong language. In the back of his head, he was crossing his mental fingers that he wasn't overplaying his cards. "Your Honor, Ms. Morris' request for such a lengthy delay is more than merely unreasonable. We believe it is both unconstitutional and unconscionable. The State's inaction has willfully blinded itself to the facts, the true facts, and now it seeks to drag its feet for no viable purpose and serves merely to keep an innocent man in prison. We all know the truism that justice delayed is justice denied. Keeping the Court from considering copious amounts of plainly exculpatory evidence for months on end certainly fits that old maxim. We ask the Court to deny the request for an extension."

It was apparent to those watching from the gallery that Judge Jackson was unmoved by the statements from either attorney. She was merely letting them make their record for the court reporter in the event one of the parties wished to appeal today's outcome. She issued her ruling without further ado or preamble. "After due consideration, the Court is persuaded it is proper to take judicial notice of what has, for better or worse, become common knowledge. The motion for a continuance is denied as the State has offered no compelling reason for delaying today's consideration."

Morris wasn't willing to take the "L" on her motion. "But Your Honor, the ..." she sputtered when Judge Jackson again interrupted her.

"Ms. Morris, there's another old maxim here that applies as well. A party with the burden of persuasion who arrives empty-handed on decision day must expect to lose. If the State disagrees strongly enough with my decision, it can file an appeal based upon the record."

Judge Jackson motioned to the briefing she held up that had been filed in advance of today's hearing as she then spoke directly to Jerry. "Mr. Tavington, it's your client's motion and briefing. Walk the Court through it, please."

As Tavington again rose from his seat to make the case that he had rehearsed in his office (while I peppered him with every objection and counterargument I could think of), Judge Jackson's last statement was still occupying my attention. What did she mean by *"it's your client's motion and briefing"*? I could see only Tavington's brief on both tables, and Judge Jackson had only held up a single brief after her reference to showing up empty-handed. Shocked, I finally understood what happened.

The State hadn't filed a responsive brief opposing the Motion that Tavington filed to overturn Martin Triton's conviction. Whether from oversight or some other strategy intended to defuse the explosive situation, the State was basically here empty-handed and Morris expected to lose. Over the next hour, Morris fought hard, but Tavington's mastery of the facts and arguments should have prevailed regardless of whether Morris' rhetorical hands had been tied. She was in the highly unenviable position of having to defend an indefensibly flawed conviction. Everyone, including Judge Jackson, knew it.

In the end, Judge Jackson ordered Martin Triton's murder conviction overturned, and she told Morris the State can elect to retry Martin using the newly uncovered evidence if the State still felt it still had a viable case against him.

The State never pursued Martin for a retrial because Tavington would have had an absolute field day. No prosecutor wanted to get buried by a mountain of exculpatory evidence. The optics of a parade of disgraced government officials going to jail for corruption continued for months, and NorthStar NewsHub's collaboration with "Murder in Minnesota" again paid rich benefits for both media outfits.

CHAPTER 23

MARCH 4

PRIOR LAKE CUPPYCAKES – PRIOR LAKE

The steam from my cup of black coffee rose lazily, the steam disappearing into the air along with the steam from Archer's mug as we sat at a table in the back of the busy store. Despite its name, *Prior Lake Cuppycakes* made much more than the cupcakes for which they were known. Right now, both of us were about to eat their excellent, gooey caramel rolls when an unexpected shadow blocked the morning's sun shining through the window that had brightly lit our table.

"I thought I'd find you here," said Detective David Deroshier as he took the open seat at our small table. "Got an update for ya." He set his cup of coffee and a pastry on the table, then looked intently at us.

"I guess we're getting predictable and easy to find nowadays," Archer quipped.

"Well … retired," I answered, as if that made the reason why perfectly obvious. "What's the story, Dave?"

"My sources at the rumor mill are telling me they've given up trying to find the guys behind the Gunfight at the OK Corral. ATF came up snake eyes in their efforts to trace the RPG to any identifiable source or end user. No one has been able to run down that plumbing van, identify who was in it or even identify the stiffs who the RPG blew into another zip code. They got nothing, and nothing has turned up that would identify anyone," Deroshier said, before sipping his cup of dark roast. He made an appreciative face at the full, but well-balanced, flavor, then took a bite of his pastry. "I can see why you guys stop here in the mornings," he added

Archer and I exchanged brief glances, and he spoke first. "Can't say we're too surprised. Seemed like a mob hit to us, but we're just looking in from the outside."

Deroshier raised an eyebrow. "Would you guys know anything about who was inv …" he started to say when Archer and I interrupted him.

"No!" we said in unison. Our unexpected vehemence clearly surprised Deroshier.

"Last thing we want to do is start banging sticks on the outside of that particular hive of sleaze and firepower. Not a healthy thing for guys like us to get mixed up in," I said.

Archer snorted. "Especially the firepower part."

Deroshier arched his eyebrows in confusion. "But, you published the stolen data," he muttered aloud. "What's the difference?"

"Making stolen data available after someone sent it to us and another media broadcaster isn't the same as those lunatics who broke in and survived the gunfight to get the hell outta there. Not by a mile," I said.

Without trading looks again, I could sense Archer was likewise pleased our cover remained intact thanks to the elaborate precautions we took to hide our identities. You can never be too sure, but it seemed like we had gotten away with it. The fact that two men died that night, plus several other persons were later killed due to the consequences of our actions to expose them was something we could live with. Both of us were too old and experienced to catch a raging case of The Sads when bad guys got their comeuppance.

Chuckling a little bit, Deroshier tilted his head to the side for a moment before he took another sip of coffee. It was his way of acknowledging defeat while also indicating he felt just as heartbroken about the dead bad guys as we did. "Well then, the Sgt. Schultz defense works well for you."

Archer chuckled. "Which defense? The one where we know nothing, saw nothing or heard nothing?"

Deroshier laughed. "Yes," he said simply, leaving us to figure it out. "By the way, we indicted the guards who were on duty when Samantha Triton and Tammy Kettle got ended. Same for the deputy warden."

I nodded. "We figured that would happen at some point. Their names had been matched to the union's payee list." Deroshier seemed unsurprised. Both "Murder in Minnesota" and NorthStar NewsHub had publicly called for them to be investigated because of the link between them all that had been well publicized.

Deroshier wasn't done. "Martin Triton might still face charges from the SEC over his espionage with Dakota Aerospace, but that's up to the feds to decide. Beats life in prison for murder, though."

After that statement, the three of us sat in companionable silence while we enjoyed our breakfast, crowd watched, and reflected on the amazing events each of us had experienced and investigated over the past year. I couldn't help but wonder what was next for us.

That thought spawned unsettling shadows to flit across my mind. The biggest tragedy in life is we get old too soon and wise too late, and there always seems to be something sinister lurking out there that we keep stumbling into.

AFTERWORD

I am incredibly appreciative that you have taken the time to read this book. I would ask you to leave a review and upvote any existing reviews you agree with, as those are critical to others considering purchasing this book.

Like most authors, I spend more time self-editing than actually writing. And everyone knows self-editing is as thoroughly exciting as watching paint dry. Despite those efforts, spelling, punctuation and grammatical errors inexorably creep and hide from my editing tools. In this era of online publishing, when appropriate I can correct such errors and update the materials.

John Filcher

Craving more investigative mysteries?
Keep an eye out for the next adventures of
Archer, Tavington, Masterson and Finch
in Book 3 of the Murder in Minnesota series.

9 781962 402149